HER ITALIAN
BOSS'S AGENDA

BY

LUCY GORDON

MILLS & BOON®

First published in Great Britain 2005
Large Print edition 2006
Harlequin Mills & Boon Limited,
Eton House, 18-24 Paradise Road,
Richmond, Surrey TW9 1SR

© Lucy Gordon 2005

ISBN 0 263 18970 8

Set in Times Roman 16½ on 18 pt.
16-0506-46861

Printed and bound in Great Britain
by Antony Rowe Ltd, Chippenham, Wiltshire

HER ITALIAN
BOSS'S AGENDA

PROLOGUE

'FEBRUARY!' Carlo sighed. 'Who needs it? Christmas is over and the best of the year hasn't started.'

'You mean there are no pretty tourists yet,' Ruggiero ribbed him. 'Don't you ever think of anything else?'

'No,' Carlo said simply. 'And you're just as bad, so don't deny it.'

'I wasn't going to.'

They were twins, not identical, but clearly brothers. Handsome, in the glory of their late twenties, they stood on the terrace of the Villa Rinucci, looking down at the Bay of Naples. It was late afternoon and darkness was falling fast. In the distance Mount Vesuvius loomed ominously, and below them the lights of the city winked.

Somewhere behind them their mother spoke.

'You would like my country, my sons. Every February, in England we celebrate the Feast of St Valentine, the patron saint of love.

Flowers, cards, kisses—you two would be in your element.'

'Instead, it's Primo going to England,' Carlo observed gloomily. 'It'll be wasted on him. All he'll think of is business.'

'Your brother works hard,' Hope Rinucci reproved them, trying to sound severe. 'You should both try it.'

This was a slander, since these young men worked as hard as they played, which was very hard indeed. But they only grinned at their mother sheepishly.

'Why does Primo have to keep taking over firms, anyway?' Ruggiero asked. 'When will he stop?'

'Come inside and eat,' Hope ordered them. 'This is Primo's farewell dinner.'

'We give him a farewell dinner every time he goes away,' Carlo objected.

'And why not? It's a good chance to get the family together,' Hope said.

'Will Luke be here tonight?' Carlo asked.

'Of course he will,' Hope declared, a little too firmly. 'I know he and Primo have the occasional argument—'

'Occasional!' the twins groaned in unison.

'All right, most of the time. But they are still brothers.'

'Not really,' Ruggiero said. 'They're not related at all.'

'Primo is my stepson and Luke is my adopted son, and that makes them brothers,' Hope said firmly. 'Is that clear?'

'Yes, Mamma,' they both said in meek voices.

Inside the house there was warmth and the comfortable bustle of a family. But Hope looked around, dissatisfied.

'There are too many men here,' she declared.

Her husband and sons looked alarmed, as though wondering by what drastic means she intended to reduce the number.

'There should be more women,' she explained. 'Where are my daughters-in-law? I should have six by now, and I have none. I was so looking forward to seeing Justin marry Evie, but—' She gave an eloquent shrug and a sigh.

Justin was her eldest son, parted from her since his birth, but reunited the previous year. He'd come to Naples once with Evie, the woman he clearly loved. But then Evie had mysteriously vanished from his life, and when he'd returned at Christmas she hadn't been with him. Nor would he speak of her.

Gradually the big dining room filled up and, despite her disapproving words, she looked around her with satisfaction. Her sons had their own apartments in Naples, and it was a great day when she could gather them together in this house.

Her eyes lit up at the sight of Primo, her stepson by her first husband, an Englishman, although he now bore the Rinucci family name in honour of his Italian mother.

'It's been too long since I've seen you,' she said, hugging him. 'And tomorrow you're going away again.'

'Not for long, Mamma. I'll soon get this English firm into shape.'

'Why did you have to buy it at all? You were doing good business with it.'

'Curtis Electronics wasn't being run properly, so I decided to take it over. Enrico wasn't keen at first, but he finally saw it my way.'

'I'm sure he did,' Hope observed wryly.

Enrico Leonate had once been the sole owner of Leonate Europa, a firm for which Primo had gone to work fifteen years ago. He had learned quickly, made a great deal of money for his boss and for himself, and eventually had become a partner. Enrico was elderly and tired. Primo was young, thrusting and full of ideas. Enrico was glad enough to let him take the reins but, as he'd once ruefully remarked, it would have been all the same if he hadn't been. Sooner or later people tended to see things Primo's way.

Now he was telling Hope, 'I'll promote a few people, and tell them what I want.'

'That's if you can find anyone there who satisfies you. Since when did anyone live up to your expectations?'

'True,' he agreed. 'But Cedric Tandy, the present manager, recommends his deputy, Olympia Lincoln. I'll watch her closely.'

'And promote a woman?' Hope asked satirically. 'You—an equal opportunity employer?'

He looked surprised. 'I'll promote anyone who'll do as I say.'

'Ah! That kind of equal opportunity.' Hope laughed. 'My son, you make it sound so simple.'

'Most of life is simple if you know what you want and are determined to get it.'

She frowned, then forgot everything in the pleasure of seeing him here. As always, he had arrived at the perfect moment, not late but not too early, and elegantly dressed.

His appearance betrayed his dual heritage. From his long-dead Italian mother he had inherited dark eyes with a wealth of varied expressions, changing from one moment to the next. His English father had bequeathed him a stubborn chin and firm mouth, lacking the Italian mobility that characterised the other men.

'Luke isn't here yet,' she said in a low voice.

'He probably isn't coming,' Primo said cheerfully. 'I'm not his favourite person since I poached Tordini.'

Rico Tordini was a brilliant electronics inventor, claimed by both brothers, whose business interests were in the same line. Primo had secured him for his own firm.

'Luke says you stabbed him in the back,' Hope reminded Primo.

'Not a bit. It's true he spotted Tordini first, but I made him a better offer.'

'My dear, it's a bad business when brothers fall out.'

'Don't worry, Mamma. Luke will get his chance of revenge, and he'll take it.'

He spoke lightly. The running battle between himself and Luke had lasted years now, and provided spice to their lives. Without it they would both have felt something was missing.

Luke finally put in an appearance when the meal was almost over.

'*E, Inglese,*' Primo said, raising his glass in jeering fashion.

To call Luke an Englishman was Primo's favourite form of insult, a way of reminding him that he was the only son in this Italian family who was completely English.

'Better than being neither one thing nor the other,' Luke said with a grin, referring to Primo's dual ancestry and the fact that he was liable to 'switch sides' without warning.

'I'm glad you came,' Hope told him.

'Naturally.' Luke raised a glass sardonically in Primo's direction. 'I had to make sure we were really getting rid of him.'

Yet it was Luke who drove Primo to the airport the next day.

'I'm coming too,' Hope told them. 'Someone has to stop you two killing each other.'

'No fear of that,' Luke said lightly. 'It's more fun to plot a subtle revenge. That's the Italian way.'

'And what would an *Inglese* know of the Italian way?' Primo demanded.

'Only what he's learned from his mongrel brother.'

As Hope and Luke stood together watching the plane climb, she couldn't help giving a little sigh.

'Don't worry, Mamma,' Luke said, his arm about her shoulders. 'He'll be back in no time.'

'It's not that. People say how lucky I am that Primo never gives me cause for worry. But I do worry, because he's *too* reliable. He's so sensible, he never does anything stupid.'

'I promise you, if he's a Rinucci, he's stupid,' Luke said fervently.

'Indeed? And what does that make you, since you've always refused to take our name?'

He hugged her. 'I don't need it. I'm stupid enough anyway.'

CHAPTER ONE

IN THE London headquarters of Curtis Electronics tensions simmered. Employees hurried in, anxious not to be late, wondering who would be promoted and who pensioned off.

'They're not getting rid of me,' Olympia Lincoln said firmly. 'Not after all the work I've put into this firm, and the plans I've made.'

'It is rotten luck, this happening now,' Sara, her secretary, said sympathetically. 'Mr Tandy was bound to retire soon, and then you'd have had his job.'

'Grr!' Olympia said with feeling.

'The worst thing is not knowing when the new people will be here.' Sara sighed.

'Right. Even Mr Tandy doesn't know. "Some time soon" is all he can say. Maybe today, maybe next week.'

'Surely not today,' Sara objected. 'It's Friday. What sort of person makes his first day a Friday?'

'Someone who's trying to catch us out,' Olympia said at once. 'I'm blowed if I'm going to let anyone take me by surprise.'

'But today isn't just Friday,' Sara objected. *'It's Friday the thirteenth.'*

'Don't tell me you're superstitious.' Olympia chuckled. 'That's nonsense. People should make their own fate.'

'But Friday the thirteenth is bad luck.'

'It'll be bad luck for Primo Rinucci if he crosses me. Now let's have some tea. I'll make it. You're looking queasy.'

'I'm fine really,' Sara said valiantly, if untruthfully. 'You shouldn't be making tea. You're the boss.'

'But you're the one who's pregnant,' Olympia said with a warm smile that transformed her face from its usual severe lines. She cultivated that severity, determined to make the world believe it. But her natural kindness had a habit of breaking through, although usually only Sara saw this and she was sworn to secrecy.

'That's better.' Sara sighed gratefully when she'd sipped the strong tea. 'Did you ever want children?'

'Once I did. When I married David I was madly in love and all I wanted was to be his wife and the mother of his children. Which probably makes me a disgrace to modern womanhood. But I was eighteen at the time, so maybe there was some excuse for me.'

'Did he appreciate this slavish devotion?'

'Did he, hell? He needed a working wife so that he could take courses and get diplomas that would help his career. When he moved onward and upward to the next promotion, plus the next wife, I was left with nothing. So I worked like the devil and made a career for myself.'

'You were unlucky, but not all men are like him.'

'Most of the ambitious ones are. They use us unless we use them first.'

'So that's what you do,' Sara agreed, regarding her boss sympathetically, and recalling various incidents in the last couple of years that now made more sense. 'Are you happy?'

'What's happy? I'm not *un*happy. I remember how I felt when David walked out, and that's never going to happen to me again. I'm going to get Tandy's job, you wait and see. I just have to work on—whoever turns up from Italy.'

'How's your Italian?'

'Not bad. I've been learning hard, but I suppose everyone else here has done the same.'

'None of the others will have prepared like you have, either in the head or the—' Sara made a gesture indicating Olympia's appearance, and Olympia laughed.

Both inside and out, her grooming was impeccable. Her mind was focused, steely. Her body was slender and elegant, clad in a blue linen dress.

She was tall for a woman, with long legs, a long neck and cleanly chiselled features. Her black hair was naturally luxuriant, but she wore it smoothed back against her head and twined into sleek braids behind.

In this she was illogical. The sensible thing would be to cut it off in a neat, boyish crop. But for once she couldn't make herself do the sensible thing. She wasn't sure why.

Her eyes were also dark, lustrous, with depths where humour still lurked occasionally, although she did her best to conceal it. She was a perfectly groomed creation, crafted to her own meticulous design.

In only one thing had she failed to achieve her own standards. At heart she knew that part of her was still the same girl she'd once been, the one she was trying to deny. That girl had been full of trust and eagerness, without a calculating bone in her body. She hadn't merely loved her husband, she'd worshipped him blindly. She'd also possessed a temper and an unruly tongue, which sometimes spoke before her mind was in gear.

All these things she'd striven to put right, and had mostly succeeded. Occasionally she was still betrayed by anger into rash speech, but she was working on that too.

Today was going to put all her skill to the test.

'Do you know who's going to turn up to look us over?' Sara asked.

'Probably Primo Rinucci. I've tried to research the firm on-line but there isn't much. There's two partners, Enrico Leonate and Primo Rinucci. I managed to find Leonate's picture on-line, but unfortunately there was no picture for Rinucci.'

'What does Signor Leonate look like?'

'Dull, middle-aged. Let's hope Primo Rinucci isn't the same.'

But even as she spoke Olympia was giving Sara a worried look.

'You're not well,' she said.

'I'll be fine in a minute.'

'Oh, no! You're going home. I don't want it on my conscience that anything went wrong with your baby.' She picked up the phone, dialled reception and ordered a taxi on the firm.

'Go home and call the doctor,' she said. 'And don't come back until you're a lot better.'

'But how will you manage without me?' Sara asked worriedly.

Olympia gave her a cheerful smile. 'I'll just have to stagger along somehow. Don't worry.'

She went down to reception, saw Sara into the waiting taxi and waved it off.

She was frowning as she returned to her office. She'd spoken reassuringly to Sara, but it was the worst possible time for this to happen.

She called Central Staff and explained that she urgently needed a temporary secretary, adding, 'the best you have. And quickly, please.'

'Someone will be there in five minutes.'

When she'd hung up Olympia took some deep breaths and closed her eyes.

'I will not let this get to me,' she said to herself. 'If things go wrong I will overcome them. I will. *I will.* I am strong. Nothing can defeat me.'

She repeated this mantra several times before opening her eyes and getting the shock of her life.

A young man was standing there, watching her with interest.

He was very tall with slightly shaggy brown hair, dark brown eyes and a wide, firm mouth. He seemed to be regarding Olympia with some amusement, but perhaps that was only her imagination. She hoped desperately that her lips hadn't been moving.

'Can I help you?' she asked coolly.

'I'm looking for Olympia Lincoln. They told me downstairs that I'd find her here.'

The Central Staff Office was downstairs. After the first surprise Olympia recovered.

Male secretaries were quite common these days.

'I am Olympia Lincoln,' she said. 'I'm glad you got here quickly. They said they'd send me a replacement in five minutes, but—' She shrugged.

'Replacement?'

'Well, not permanent replacement, of course. Just temporary until my regular secretary is feeling better. Have you been here long—with the firm, I mean?'

'No, a very short time,' he said. He was watching her keenly and picking his words with caution.

'Never mind, you'll soon get the hang of it. We're in the middle of an upheaval at the moment. Curtis has been taken over by an Italian firm called Leonate Europa, and soon someone will arrive from Italy to make it official. We're all waiting in fear and trembling to learn our fate.'

He raised his eyebrows. 'Fear and trembling? You?'

She gave a half smile, pleased by the implication. 'Yes—well—I can do a good imitation of it if necessary.'

'Will it be necessary?'

'I'll tell you that when I've met His Majesty.'

'Who's he?'

'Primo Rinucci. The "great man" who's coming to whip us all into line. Damned cheek!'

'Isn't it a bit soon to blame him? He might be all right.'

Suddenly her carefully cultivated pose fractured under the burden of her anger.

'He's not all right. He's a predator who thinks he can snatch whatever he wants and to hell with everyone else. Ooh, I wish he was here so that I can give him a piece of my mind!'

'It's only a moment ago you were going to pretend to fear and tremble.'

'I'll do that first. *Then* I'll tell him what I think of him, coming here, disrupting my life, taking my promotion just when it's in my grasp, thinking his money can buy anything.'

'Money has a way of doing that,' he observed mildly. 'It's one of its virtues.'

'To hell with virtue, to hell with money and to hell with Primo Rinucci.'

The sight of her eyes, blazing with indignation, held him entranced. Men had lost their heads for eyes like that, he thought. As he was in danger of doing.

'I can see that this is going to be a meeting of Titans,' he murmured.

She returned to sanity, and sighed.

'Well, keep what you've just heard to yourself. I suppose I shouldn't have spoken so freely in front of you—'

'My lips are sealed,' he promised. 'I swear never to tell Primo Rinucci what you really think of him.'

'Thank you, but be careful. Since we don't know what he looks like, you might find yourself talking to him without knowing it's him. He's probably the sort of low life who'd keep his identity secret just to be mean.'

'Yes,' he said, with a touch of guilt. 'I suppose that's possible.'

'But then, his being Italian would be a giveaway.'

'Maybe not,' he couldn't resist saying. 'Not all Italians say *Mamma mia!* and wave their hands. In fact, I believe some of them are indistinguishable from normal human beings.'

Try as he might, he couldn't keep a note of irony out of his voice. Luckily she was too preoccupied to notice.

'But he'd have an accent,' she persisted. 'He wouldn't sound English like you and me.'

He cleared his throat, then seemed to go into a kind of trance. In truth he was struggling with a temptation more overwhelming than any he'd known in his life. A wise man would tell her the truth before it was too late.

But it was already too late, and never had he felt so reluctant to be wise.

'By the way, I should have asked your name,' Olympia said.

He played for time.

'What?' he asked vaguely.

'Your name.'

'My name.'

'That's right. What is it—your name?'

She spoke patiently, and her eyes showed that she thought she was dealing with a half-wit. Was that better than telling her that he was Primo Rinucci?

For one wild moment he teetered on the brink of the truth.

Tell her who you really are. Be honest. Play safe.

He took a deep breath. To blazes with honesty! As for safety—nuts to it!

'Jack Cayman,' he said.

It had been the name of his English father. It was many years now that he'd lived in Italy as a Rinucci. But his early years had left their mark, and he could still speak English without a trace of Italian accent. So it was easy for him, now, to look Olympia in the eye and claim to be Jack Cayman.

She extended her hand. 'Well, Mr Cayman—'

'You can call me Jack.'

'You can call me Miss Lincoln,' she said firmly, feeling that it was time she reclaimed the ground she'd lost in that burst of frankness.

'Yes, ma'am,' he said meekly.

'Now, the sooner we get down to work the better.'

'Would you just give me a few minutes first?' he asked hurriedly. 'I'll be straight back.'

'Of course. It's just down the corridor on the right.'

'Thanks,' he said, hurrying out of the door.

It was several moments before it dawned on him that she'd directed him to the gentlemen's convenience.

For the past week Cedric Tandy had been in his office half an hour early, so it was plain misfortune that when the crucial day came he was half an hour late.

'Oh no,' he moaned at the sight of the man waiting for him. 'Signor Rinucci—I assure you—'

'It's all right, Cedric,' Primo said pleasantly. 'I just thought I'd drop in for a chat.'

'Perhaps I can show you around and introduce you—'

'That can come later. I've been looking over the financial arrangements Enrico and I made for you, and it struck me that they were rather on the mean side. I'm sure you deserve something more generous.'

'Well—that's very good to hear but—Signor Leonate said that your firm couldn't pay any more—'

'You leave him to me. If he won't fund an increase I'll do it myself.'

Cedric gaped as Primo walked to the door and looked back.

'By the way,' he said, as if something had only just occurred to him, 'I'd rather nobody knew who I was, just at first. They think I'm Jack Cayman. It'll give me a chance to meet people in a more spontaneous manner. I know you'll back me up.'

Cedric might not be a genius at running a company but he'd learned shrewdness. He understood bribery. But he also understood about gift horses.

'Count on me,' he said.

Olympia looked up from the computer as he entered her office.

'You'd better come and study these files,' she said. 'They'll tell you a lot about how Curtis and Leonate have interacted since they started doing business a year ago.'

'I think it was actually more like fifteen months,' he said. 'It began when Curtis tendered to manufacture a new kind of computer plug.'

'Excellent,' she said. 'You've been doing your homework.' She rose and indicated for him to sit at the computer. 'Are you familiar with this system?'

'I think so,' he said, choosing his words with care. It was the same as the system in use at Leonate's head office in Naples and in all their other firms, and Curtis had adopted it recently at his own 'urgent recommendation.'

'I think it's a pain in the neck,' she said with a touch of annoyance. 'Our old system was much better, but Leonate insisted on this one so that we can network with their other companies.'

'Is it really a pain in the neck, or do you just hate your new bosses?' he asked with a faint grin.

'I can't afford to hate them.'

'But if you could, you would, huh?'

'I think I'd better not answer that. Let me explain how this all fits together.'

She proceeded to give him a run-down of the firm and its relations with Leonate. Her mind was clear and well-informed, and she had details at her fingertips. When his umpteenth attempt to trip her up failed he admitted to himself that he was impressed.

He had also to admit that he was finding it hard to concentrate through the distraction of her perfume. At first he hadn't been sure she was wearing any, so subtle and mysterious was it. But at close range the muted aroma just reached him, then faded, returned, faded again, teasing him with uncertainty.

The aroma, if there was one, was unlike anything he'd known before. He was used to women who dabbed on hot musk to entice him, but this had a cool, restrained quality that was almost like winter. Winter about to become spring, he thought: sweet-smelling fires in the snow, the smoke blown hither and thither, always on the verge of vanishing, always lingering.

The phone rang and she answered quickly.

'Sara? What's the news?'

'I'm in hospital,' came Sara's voice. 'It'll be months before I can work. I'm sorry, Olympia.'

'Don't worry about anything. If the baby's all right, that's what counts.'

'Bless you.'

Olympia replaced the receiver thoughtfully. Primo was watching her face.

'Your secretary's not coming back?' he asked.

'It seems not. In which case—'

She looked up as a shadow appeared in the doorway and a neat young woman hurried in.

'Miss Lincoln? I'm so sorry not to have got here earlier—'

'Was I expecting you?'

'Central Staff sent me. They said you needed a secretary.'

'But—' She gave a quick look at Primo, who let out his breath uneasily. 'But you—'

'It's a bit complicated,' he hedged.

'Will you wait outside, please?' she asked the newcomer pleasantly.

When the young woman had gone she faced him.

'I think you have some explaining to do. Just who are you?'

'I told you, my name is Jack Cayman.'

'But who is Jack Cayman? And why did he claim to be my secretary when he wasn't?'

'Ah, be fair. I never actually said that's who I was. You jumped to a conclusion.'

'Which you did nothing to correct.'

'You didn't give me a chance. You informed me why I was there, snapped your fingers, and I said, ''Yes, ma'am, anything you say, ma'am.'' And let's face it, that's the kind of answer you prefer.'

He knew this was an exaggeration, but he was fighting with his back to the wall. Anything was better than the truth.

Or was it? This could be his last chance to make a fresh start. He took a deep breath, but before he could speak a voice from the doorway sealed his fate.

'Jack, my dear fellow, how good to see you!'

It was Cedric Tandy, advancing on him, smiling, playing his allotted part.

He made some reply. He had no idea what it was. Inwardly he was cursing.

'I see you've met Olympia,' Cedric burbled on, oblivious to the wreckage he was causing. 'That's good—excellent.'

'Oh, yes, we've met,' Olympia said with glassy-eyed courtesy. 'But we were still sorting out who's who.'

'I hadn't explained who I am and where I come from,' Primo said, giving Cedric a glance fierce enough to silence him. 'It's a bit difficult to—you might call me a sort of ambassador, an outrider, sent to prepare the land before the big guns arrive.'

'And was coming to my office a part of preparing the land?' Olympia asked with deadly brightness.

'Your name has been mentioned as one of the assets of the firm,' he said. 'Now we've talked I can see I'm going to rely on you for a lot of information. Perhaps the three of us can have lunch together, and exchange views.'

'Wonderful idea!' Cedric exclaimed.

'You're very kind,' Olympia said coolly, 'but I'm afraid my lunch will be an apple at my desk. I've got a new secretary starting today, and I have to work with her.'

Cedric, aghast at this cavalier treatment of a man who came from the seat of power, began to mutter urgently, 'Olympia, I really think—'

'Naturally I respect your decision,' Primo interposed smoothly. 'Some other time. Cedric, why don't we go somewhere and talk?'

The two of them departed, leaving Olympia to reflect that she'd made a mess of everything, and it was all his fault.

She wanted to bang her head against the wall.

Or his.

Before leaving, Olympia looked in on Cedric, who informed her cheerfully that the newcomer had left an hour ago.

And he hadn't tried to talk to her again. Which meant that it wasn't just a mess. It was a complete and total mess. She ground her teeth.

In the firm's car park she headed for her new car, a prized possession whose gleaming lines usually brought her comfort. She surveyed them for a moment, trying to take the usual pleasure in this sign of success, but tonight something was out of kilter, as if a genie had threatened to rub a lamp the wrong way and snatch it all back.

Beneath her calm she was furious, more with herself than anyone else. Her plans had been laid so carefully. Primo Rinucci would arrive to find her one step ahead of him, which, of course, he would never suspect. She would play him like a fish on a line, as she had done before, although never when there was so much to win and lose.

And she'd blown it. Caught off-guard, she'd revealed her true feelings, something *you just didn't do!* Not if you wanted to reach the top as badly as she did.

Now he knew, and he would report back that she was not only stupid enough to mistake his identity, but hostile to her new employers. Great!

As she pulled out of the line and headed for the exit she became aware that another car had slipped in behind her. It followed her out on to the road and remained on her tail, keeping a safe distance, but definitely following. Glancing into her mirror she caught a glimpse of the driver and drew in a sharp breath. Him again!

Two impulses warred within her. One said this man came from the Leonate Head Office and she should be charming and recover lost ground.

The other said punch his lights out.

She compromised.

Half a mile later the road broadened out and she took the chance to draw into the kerb, get out and face him.

'Are you following me?' she demanded.

'Yes,' he admitted. 'I meant to catch up with you in the car park, but I just missed you. I thought we could talk.'

'You couldn't simply have suggested a meeting?'

'And get comprehensively snubbed? I don't think my fragile ego could stand it a second time in one day.'

'Fragile my foot!' she fumed. 'We "talked" this morning, and I'm still regretting it. You practised a wicked deception on me—'

'Not wicked,' he pleaded. 'Foolish, I grant you. I was stupid, it was a joke that went wrong, but when you just assumed that I was your secretary—well, can you blame me for playing along?'

'Yes,' she said firmly. 'It was unprofessional.'

'And not checking the facts was the height of professionalism, I suppose?' he said, stung. 'No, look, I'm sorry I said that. I don't want to turn this into a fight.'

'Then you're several hours too late. It became a fight the moment you thought I was there for your entertainment and tricked me into saying things that—' She shuddered as she recalled her incautious words.

'I didn't force you to say that stuff about "His Majesty" like "To hell with Primo Rinucci!" You were bursting to say it to some-one.'

The stark truth of this didn't improve her temper.

'And I said it to you, thus finishing my prospects with my new employers.'

'I never said—'

'You didn't have to. If you don't tell them now you'll have to warn them later, otherwise they'll find out what you knew and your own prospects will be in danger.'

'Don't worry about my prospects,' he said coolly. 'I have the virtue of thinking before I speak. It's a great help. For an ambitious woman you have a remarkably careless tongue.'

'How was I to know that you—?' She bit back the last words.

'Wasn't an underling?' he finished. 'If I *had* been the worm beneath your feet that you clearly thought, it wouldn't have mattered, would it?'

'I'm not going to dignify that with an answer,' she seethed.

'Which is probably wise! No, look—forget I said that. I'm tired, jet lagged—'

'How can you be jet lagged from Naples?' she scoffed.

'The damned plane was delayed,' he yelled. 'It didn't get in until past midnight, and I got no sleep last night. I'm not at my best, and I'm saying things I shouldn't. You're not the only one who can do that.

'So let's put an end to this now. I apologise—for everything. And I'd like to apologise properly over dinner.'

'No, thank you,' she said crisply. 'I have plans for this evening. I intend to spend it reading a book called *How To Spot A Phoney At Fifty Paces*. I thought I was good at that, but evidently I have much to learn.'

'I could give you some pointers.'

'No, you come under the heading of practical experience. After you I need further instruction. I'll probably take a crash course, with a diploma at the end of it.'

'I really screwed up, didn't I?' He sighed.

'Need you ask? Now, Mr Cayman, if you'll excuse me, I have to get home. I suggest you turn around and spend the evening writing a report for your employers. Be sure to include *everything*.'

'That's not how I plan to spend my evening.'

'If you follow me again I'll call the police.'

'What for? Surely you can deal with this situation without help. I'd back you against the police any day.'

'That was an entirely unnecessary observation.'

'I thought I was paying you a compliment.'

'Then we have different ideas about what constitutes a compliment. *Goodnight!*'

CHAPTER TWO

WITHOUT waiting for a reply, Olympia got back into her car and started up with a vigour that threatened to finish off the engine. Primo sighed, returned to his own car and pulled out.

What happened next was something he was never quite able to analyse, except to say that he was still mentally in Italy, where drivers used the other side of the road, and the steering was on the other side of the car. In daylight he might have coped better, but with lights glaring at him out of the darkness he briefly lost his sense of direction. The next thing he knew was an ugly scraping sound of metal on metal and a hefty clout on the head.

He swore, more at the indignity than the pain.

Olympia appeared, pulling open his door. 'Oh, great. All I need is a clown to ram my new car—hey, are you all right?'

'Sure, fine,' he lied, blinking and making a vain effort to clear his head.

'You don't look it. You look as if you were seeing stars. Did you hit your head?'

'Just a little bump. What about you? Are you hurt?'

'No, my car took all the damage. There's not a scratch on me.'

He got out, moving slowly because his head was swimming, and surveyed what he could see of the dent. There was no doubt who had hit whom, he thought, annoyed with himself for ceding a point to her.

'I'm sorry,' he groaned.

'Never mind that now. Let's get you to a hospital.'

'What for?'

'Your head needs looking at.'

'It's just a scratch. I don't want any hospital.'

'You've got to—' She checked herself. 'All right, but I'm not letting you out of my sight for a while. You can come home with me. No—' she added quickly as he turned back to the car. 'You're not driving in that state. I'll take you.'

'I don't want to abandon my car here.'

'We're not going to. If you hold a torch, I'll fix the tow.'

'Shouldn't it be me fixing the tow?'

'You've had a bump on the head. Do as I ask and don't speak.'

'Anything you say.'

He had to admit she knew what she was doing, attaching the two vehicles as efficiently as a mechanic. In no time at all they were on their way. Ten minutes drive brought them to a smart block of flats, where Olympia parked both cars efficiently.

'I'll call the hire firm first thing tomorrow,' he said, adding wryly, 'They'll be thrilled.'

'When did you hire it?'

'This morning.'

Her apartment was on the second floor. It was neat, elegant and expensively furnished with perfect taste, he noticed, but it seemed to him that there was something lacking. For the moment he couldn't define it.

'Sit down while I look at your forehead,' she said.

Unwilling though he was to admit it, his head was aching horribly, and a glance in the mirror showed him a nasty bruise and some scratches that were bleeding.

'It won't take a moment for me to clean that up,' she said. 'And I'll make you a strong coffee.'

He was glad to sit down and close his eyes. From somewhere in the distance he thought he heard her talking, but then he opened his eyes to find her standing there with coffee.

'Drink this,' she said.

'Thanks. Then I'll call a taxi to take me back to my hotel. I'm sorry about your car. I'll pay for all the repairs.'

'No need. The insurance will take care of it.'

'No, I'll do it,' he said hastily, with visions of form-filling and having to give his real name. 'We don't want to damage your no-claims bonus, and I'd rather the world didn't hear about this.'

'You think they might laugh?' she asked.

'Fit to bust,' he said gloomily.

The coffee was good. Almost up to Italian standard.

As he was finishing it there was a knock at the door. Olympia answered it and returned with a young man.

'This is Dr Kenton,' she said. 'I called him when we came in.'

He groaned. 'I told you I'm all right.'

'Why not let me decide that?' the doctor asked pleasantly.

He studied the bruise for a few moments, then took out an instrument which he used to look into his patient's eyes, before declaring, 'Mild concussion. It's not serious but you ought to go straight to bed and have a good sleep.'

'I'll go home right now,' he said, giving Olympia a reproachful look.

'Is there anyone there to look after you?' the doctor asked.

'Not really,' Olympia said. 'It's a hotel. That's why he's staying here.'

'Nonsense—' Primo protested.

'He's staying here,' Olympia repeated, as though he hadn't spoken.

'Ah, good.' Dr Kenton looked from one to the other. 'That's all right, is it? I mean, you two are—'

'The best of enemies,' Olympia said cheerfully. 'Never fear, I'll keep him in the land of the living. I haven't had such a promising fight on my hands for ages.'

Dr Kenton grinned and produced some pills from his bag.

'Put him to bed and give him a couple of these,' he said. 'I'll see myself out.'

When they were alone they looked at each other wryly for a moment until Primo said, 'If I'd thought about it for a month beforehand I could hardly have made a bigger foul-up, could I?'

'True,' she said, amused. 'But don't knock it. It's left me feeling so much in charity with you.'

He managed a faint laugh. 'Yes, there's nothing like having the other feller at a disadvantage to improve your mood.'

'There's a supermarket next door. I'll just go along and get some things for you, then I'll make up your bed when I get back. Don't even think of leaving while I'm gone.'

'Don't worry. I couldn't.'

In the supermarket she went swiftly round the shelves taking shaving things, socks and underwear. She had to guess the size but it wasn't hard. Tall, lean, broad-shouldered. Just the way she liked a man to be. Evidently her subconscious had been taking notes.

She looked for pyjamas too, but the supermarket's clothes range was limited to small items. Finally she stocked up on some extra groceries and hurried back, only half believing his promise to stay there.

But she found him stretched out on her sofa, his eyes closed, and got to work without disturbing him, putting clean sheets on her own bed, as there was no guest room.

'How did I get into this?' she asked herself. 'It's only an hour ago I was planning dire vengeance.'

When she returned to the main room he was awake and looking around vaguely.

'The bed's ready,' she told him.

'I'm afraid I don't have any night things.'

'That's all right. I got you some stuff in the supermarket. You'll find it in there.'

'Thanks. You've been very kind. I can manage now.'

His head was aching badly and he was glad to find the bedroom in semi-darkness, with only a small bedside lamp lit. When she was safely out of the room he removed his clothes and pulled on the boxer shorts she'd provided, meaning to don the vest as well. He would just lie down for a moment first.

It was bliss to put his head on the soft pillow and feel the ache slip gently away in sleep.

Olympia slept on the sofa. Waking in the early hours, she sat up, listening intently to the silence. There wasn't a sound, but a faint crack of light under her bedroom door told her that the lamp was still on.

Frowning, she went over to the door and hesitated only a moment before turning the handle quietly and looking inside. Then she stopped.

His clothes were on the floor, tossed everywhere, as though he'd only just torn them off before sleep overcame him. He'd put on the underpants, but not the vest, which was still loosely clasped in one hand as he lay on his back, his head turned slightly aside, his arms outstretched.

At first she viewed him with concern, in case he wasn't recovering properly. But then she realised that he was breathing easily, relaxed and contented. All was well.

It was lucky for him, she thought, that she wasn't the kind of woman to take advantage of a defenceless man; otherwise she would have let her eyes linger on his chest, smooth and muscular, and his long arms and legs. Propriety demanded that she withdraw, after she'd switched off the lamp.

Moving carefully, she eased herself along the side of the bed and reached for the switch. The sudden darkness seemed to disturb him for he muttered something and rolled over on the bed, flinging out an arm so that it brushed against her thigh.

She stood petrified, not wanting him to awaken and find her here, but realising that movement would be difficult. Between the large bed and the large wardrobe was a space too narrow for her to back away from his hand. Holding her breath, she took hold of his fingers, turning them enough for her to slip past.

But when she tried to let go she found that she couldn't. Suddenly his fingers tightened on hers. She twisted her hand, but it only made him clasp her more strongly.

Holding her breath, she dropped to her knees and put up her free hand, trying to release herself gently. A shaft of light from the window showed her his face, very near to hers, outlining the mouth that seemed different now. Earlier, she'd seen in it strength and a kind of jeering confidence, almost laughing at her even when he was trying to placate her.

But now, with its lines relaxed, it seemed softer, gentler, as though its smiles came naturally, and its laughter might be more real and spontaneous. Even delightful.

She drew a swift breath and rose to her feet, pulling her hand free and leaving the room without a backward glance.

Primo awoke suddenly. The pain in his head had completely gone and he was filled with a sense of well-being stronger than he had ever known before. It had something to do with the extraordinary woman who'd appeared in his life the day before and caused him to behave like a stranger to himself.

Lying there gazing into the darkness, not sure exactly where he was or how he'd got there, he wondered if he would ever recognise himself again. And decided that he wouldn't greatly mind if he didn't.

But then, he'd never quite recognised himself in all the years he'd had a dual identity.

He couldn't remember his mother, Elsa Rinucci, dead only a few weeks after his birth. In fact his earliest clear memory was of standing in the register office, aged four, while his father married a nineteen-year-old girl called Hope.

He'd adored her and had been on tenterhooks in case the wedding fell through. Only when it was over had he felt safe in his possession of a mother.

But no possession was eternally safe, he'd discovered. After two years, Hope and Jack had adopted Luke. He was a year younger than Primo, which everyone thought was charming.

'They'll be such companions for each other.'

And they had been, after a fashion. When they hadn't been squabbling and sabotaging each other's childish projects, they had formed an alliance against the world. But it had been an uneasy alliance, always ready to fracture.

His cruellest memory was of having his heart broken when he was nine years old. Jack and Hope's marriage ended in divorce, and she had departed, taking Luke but not himself. Only much later had he understood that she'd had no choice. He was Jack's son, but not hers. She could claim custody of Luke, but Primo had to be left with his father, feeling deserted by the only mother he had ever known.

There he had remained until Jack's death two years later, when his Rinucci relatives had taken him to live in Naples. To his joy, Hope had come to find him. That was how she'd met his Uncle Toni, and their marriage had soon followed.

Primo had taken the family name, and for a long time now had thought of himself as a Rinucci from Naples. But with the beautiful, maddening, fascinating woman whose bed he was occupying, that was the one person he couldn't be.

It was seven a.m., still dark at that time of the year, yet late enough for him to be thinking of rising. Pulling on his trousers, he went to the door and opened it a crack. It was still dark but a glow was beginning to come through a window, illuminating the young woman who stood there.

For a moment he didn't recognise her. This mysterious creature with the long black hair streaming down over her shoulders, over her breasts, halfway down her back, was quite different from the austere woman he'd met by day. The pale grey light limned her softly, bleaching colours away until she was all shadows.

She was looking out into the growing light as though the dawn itself was bringing her to life. She was growing brighter, more real, yet without losing her mystery.

Una strega, he thought, using the Italian word for a witch.

He was thinking not of an old crone stirring a cauldron, but of a temptress, endlessly enticing, teasing her prey to follow her to a place where anything could happen. Italian legends were full of such creatures, alarming even in their beauty, impossible to resist. With that long black hair she seemed to be one of them, plotting spells of darkness and light. A man who wanted the answer would have to follow her into the dancing shadows. And then it would be too late.

He shook his head, astonished at himself for such thoughts. He prided himself on his good sense and here he was, indulging in fantasies about witches.

But how could a man help it when faced with her fascinating contradictions? She showed an austere aspect to the world, scraping back her hair against her skull in a no-nonsense fashion and sleeping in pyjamas.

Nor were they seductive pyjamas. There was nothing frilly or baby-doll about them, no embroidery or lace. And she probably hadn't even realised that light from the right angle would shine through the thin material, revealing the outline of high, firm breasts, narrow waist and delicately flared hips. If she'd known that she would probably have worn flannel, he realised despondently.

He forced himself reluctantly back to earth and looked around the dimly lit room. When he saw the sofa with its pillows and blankets, it dawned on him that she'd slept there, while he occupied her bed.

He ought to move away. No gentleman would watch her while she was unaware, standing in a light that almost made her naked. So he limited himself to another two minutes before forcing himself to back off, closing the door silently.

He waited another few minutes, putting on his shirt and making plenty of noise to warn her. When he opened the door again he saw that the sofa had been stripped of sheets and blankets.

Olympia emerged from the kitchen, smiling. She was dressed in sweater and trousers and her hair was still long, although it had been drawn back and held by a coloured scarf.

'Good morning,' she said brightly. If he'd been thinking straight he might have thought the brightness rather forced, but he was long past thinking straight.

'How are you this morning?' she asked.

'A lot better for that sleep, thank you. In fact, thank you for everything, starting with making me come home with you. You were right about the hotel. It's a crowded place, but it would have been just like being alone.'

'Of course, you could always have asked them to send for a doctor,' she mused. 'But you wouldn't have done that. Too sensible. Men never do the sensible thing.'

'Actually, I usually do,' he said, making a face. 'That's my big problem, according to my mother. She keeps choosing wives for me but, according to her, I'm so sensible I drive them off. I tell her that when I'm ready to marry I'll find a woman as sensible as myself, and then neither of us will notice how boring the other one is.'

She laughed. From where she was standing no man had ever seemed less boring. A shaft of sunlight was falling on him, emphasising a masculine vigour that made him stand out vividly in her too-neat apartment. She found herself thinking of the countryside in summer, fierce heat, vibrant colours, everything deeper, more intense.

But the subtext of the story was that he had no wife at home. It alarmed her to find that she was glad to know that. It could make no possible difference to her. And yet she was glad.

She covered herself by turning it into a joke.

'You're in luck. I know several boring ladies who'd overlook a few deficiencies and make do with you.'

'Thank you, ma'am,' he said ironically. 'And while I'm thanking you I'll add the fact that you called the doctor last night, despite what I said. It was sneaky, but it was also the right thing to do.'

'Oh, I don't waste time arguing. When a man's totally wrong I just ignore him.'

'Now, that I believe.'

They laughed and she said, 'The bathroom's over there.'

He went in, taking the things she'd bought him, and had to admit that even her choice of shaving cream and aftershave were perfect. This was one very organised lady, who got every decision right.

But that was just one side of her, he realised. There was another side, with an unruly tongue that burst out despite all her efforts at control. That was the interesting side, the one he wanted to know more about, which was going to be hard, because it was the one she strove most fiercely to hide. But he wasn't going to give up now.

When he came out the room was empty and he could hear her moving in the kitchen. He looked around her apartment and again had the sense of something missing. Now he realised what it was. Like herself, the place was neat, focused, perfectly ordered. But what else was she? What were her dreams and desires? There was nothing here to tell him.

He could find only one thing that suggested a personal life and that was a photograph of an elderly couple, their heads close together, smiling broadly. The woman bore a faint resemblance to Olympia. Grandparents, he thought. There were no other pictures.

Her books might give a clue. But here again there was nothing helpful. Self-improvement tomes lined the shelves, courses for this, reading for that. They had been placed there by the woman who wore mannish pyjamas and sleeked her hair back, not the witch whose black locks streamed down like water.

She emerged with hot tea. 'Drink this, you'll feel better. I hope you're hungry.'

'Starving.'

From the kitchen came the sound of a toaster throwing up slices at the same moment that there was a ring on the front doorbell.

'Answer it for me, would you?' she said, heading back to the kitchen.

At the door he found a young man in a uniform, clutching a large bouquet of red roses, a bottle of champagne and a sheaf of envelopes.

'This stuff has just arrived on the desk downstairs,' he said. 'There's a few others, mind you. The post's always heavy on St Valentine's Day, but the others are nothing to Miss Lincoln's. It's the same every year.'

'OK, I'll take them.'

The roses were of the very best, heavy with perfume, clearly flown in expensively from some warmer location. He managed to read the card.

To the one and only, the girl who transformed the world.

He returned to the main room just as she appeared from the kitchen.

'You seem to be very popular,' he said.

He was stunned by the look that came over her face as she saw the roses. Her smile was tender, brilliant, beautiful with love.

'Who are they from?' he couldn't resist asking.

'What's the name on the card?' she said with a laugh.

'There's no name,' he said, and could have kicked himself for revealing that he'd read it.

'Well, if he wants to keep his identity a secret,' she said carelessly, 'who am I to say otherwise?'

'There's a bottle of champagne and several cards.'

'Thank you.' She took them and laid them aside.

'You're not even going to read them?'

She shrugged. 'What's the need? None of them will be signed.'

'Then how will you know who sent them?'

'I shall just have to guess. Now, let's eat.'

Breakfast was grapefruit, cereal and coffee, which suited him exactly. While he was eating she relented enough to put the red roses in a vase, but seemed content to leave the cards unopened.

Could any woman be so truly indifferent? he wondered. Were her admirers really surplus to requirements?

Or was this another facet of her personality?

But she was a witch, he remembered, a *strega magica,* changing before his eyes to bemuse and mystify him. And he had no choice but to follow where she led.

CHAPTER THREE

OVER coffee he said, 'Considering the mess I made of your car last night, you'd have been quite justified to have abandoned me to my fate.'

'Yes, I would,' she said promptly. 'I can't think why I didn't.'

'Perhaps you're a warm-hearted, forgiving person?'

She considered this seriously before dismissing it.

'That doesn't sound like me at all. There must be some other reason.'

'Maybe you preferred to keep me around so that you could inflict dire retribution?'

'*That* sounds much more like me,' she said triumphantly. 'How did you come to have such a nasty accident?'

'I forgot that the English drive on the wrong side of the road.'

His droll manner made her laugh again, but then she said, 'You really do spend most of your time in Italy, then?'

'A good deal. I'm at home in many places.'

'And you're part of Leonate, and that's why you're over here?'

'Uh-huh!' he said vaguely.

'And then you have to report back?'

'I shall certainly describe what I find, but I think, for the sake of my dignity, I'd better leave yesterday's events out of it. I wasn't trying to trap you. I just acted on impulse. I have a peculiar sense of humour.'

'I have no sense of humour at all,' Olympia said at once.

'That would account for it,' he said. 'I'll make a note of that for my report.' He pretended to write, reciting the words slowly. 'No—sense—of—humour—at—all.' He seemed to think for a moment before adding, 'Problem—to—be—considered—at—later—date. Suggest—dinner. Then—duck.'

'Get outa here,' she said, laughing reluctantly.

'Do you mean that literally?'

'No, I guess you can finish your breakfast first.'

They shared a grin, and he wished Luke could have been here to see him now. Luke often accused him of having no sense of humour, and that was true enough—with any other woman.

But this one brought laughter welling up inside him, filling the world with light and warmth. It was strange that she could be a witch as well, but he would solve that mystery later. Or maybe he would never solve it. For the moment he just wanted to be here.

'So what do you say?' he asked.

'About what?'

'About dinner. Shall I duck, or make a reservation at the Atelli Hotel?'

She was impressed by the name of London's newest luxury hotel.

'That sounds delightful,' she said. 'But only if you're well enough to go out.'

'I'm fine now. We'll have to see about the cars this morning. Where do you take yours for repairs?'

'There's a good place about a mile away. Are you sure about paying?'

'Quite sure,' he said firmly. 'Enough of that. Aren't you going to open those Valentine cards?'

He had resolved not to ask, but his will, so often a source of pride to him, seemed suddenly to be pitifully weak.

'I guess I might,' she said casually.

The first one was an elaborate confection of red satin and lace which had clearly cost a fortune. The message inside read,

I'll never forget. Will you?

He glanced at her face, but beyond a faint smile it revealed nothing.

Slowly she opened the other two. Both were large with pictures of flowers. Neither bore a name or a message.

But her face changed as she looked at them, growing soft, tender, with a smile that was pure delight. When he spoke to her she didn't hear him at first.

'I'm sorry, what was that?' she asked, sounding as if she'd been awoken from a dream.

'I said, you obviously know the two guys who sent those cards.'

'I know who sent them, yes,' she agreed, hoping he wouldn't notice how she'd changed the words.

'And they must feel fairly sure that—I mean—'

'They're both people I'm very fond of, and they know that.'

'Yes, that's what I figured. But doesn't it get a bit complicated?'

'Why should it?'

'Well—do they know about each other?'

'Of *course* they do. What do you take me for?'

He was beginning to wonder.

'Which one of them sent the flowers?'

Olympia shrugged mischievously.

She made no further comment, but when she rose to go to the kitchen she lingered a moment to caress the velvety roses and inhale their scent with her eyes closed and a look of exhilaration on her face.

'I'll go and get ready,' he said abruptly.

When the bedroom door had closed behind him she slipped into the bathroom and took out her cellphone, which she'd made sure of taking with her. Before dialling she turned on the water so that there was just enough noise to muffle her words.

She heard the ringing tone, then a familiar male voice. 'Hallo!'

'Dad? They're beautiful.'

'Ah, they got there.' His voice faded as he turned away and she heard him say, 'They arrived OK,' followed by a woman's squeal of excitement.

'And the cards,' she said. 'They're both lovely, but you shouldn't be so extravagant.'

'We couldn't decide between them, so we sent both.'

'You're mad, the pair of you.' She chuckled. 'What other parents send their daughter Valentine cards?'

'Well, like we said, darling, you changed the world, being born like that, when we'd given up hope. Here, your Mum wants to talk.'

Her mother's cheerful voice came down the line. 'Do you really like them, darling?'

'It's lovely, Mum—as always. But what about you?'

'Oh, I got roses too.'

'So I should hope.'

'And next year—maybe there'll be a real young man.' Her mother's voice was hopeful.

'Oh, I know you said never again, but your father and I are keeping our fingers crossed.'

'Don't hope for too much, Mum. You married the only decent guy around. After Dad they broke the mould.' Then an imp of mischief made her add, 'Actually, there's one here now.'

'You mean a man who stayed the night?'

'Yes.'

'In your bed?' Her mother sounded thrilled.

'*Mum!* You're nearly seventy. You're supposed to be old-fashioned and puritanical and tell me to save it for marriage.'

'Your Dad and I didn't. Anyway, one must move with the times.'

'Yes, he was in my bed, but don't get too excited. There's only one bed in the apartment and he had a concussion so I looked after him, and that's all.'

'Is he good-looking?'

'That really has nothing to do with it.'

'Oh, nonsense dear! It has *everything* to do with it.'

'Well—all right, yes, he's good-looking.'

'As how?'

'He's in his late thirties, tall and—well, his eyes are—really quite something.'

'What did he think about your cards and flowers?'

'He was—interested.'

'You didn't tell him they were from your parents, did you?'

Olympia chuckled. 'Nope. You taught me that much savvy.'

'That's right. Keep him guessing. Oh, this is lovely. I must tell your father. He'll be so excited.'

'Mum, you've got a wicked mind.'

'Of course, dear. It makes life so much more interesting. Are you going to see him again?'

'We're having dinner tonight.'

'*Harold!*' her mother shrieked. '*Guess what!*'

There was an indistinct mumbling, followed by her father's bellow of, 'Best of luck, darling!'

She hung up feeling happier, as she always did when talking to her parents. She could never quite figure out how those two had come this far without discovering that love and marriage were snares for fools. She only prayed that they never did discover it.

For herself, it was too late to forget what she had learned. The finer feelings were not for her. There was ambition, and there was having a good time. Tonight she was going to enjoy them both. Jack Cayman was charming company, although it was true, as she'd told her mother, that his good looks were an irrelevance.

But what really mattered was that he came from the centre of power; he would know Primo Rinucci and could tell her how to aim for her goal. Tough times and hard work lay ahead, but a person could have some fun in the meantime, couldn't she?

She had a small twinge of conscience that perhaps she was being unfair to him, but only a small one. This was how the game was played.

She was really looking forward to dinner that evening.

As he gathered his things together, ready to leave, Primo was aware of an extra presence inside his head. He knew it was his conscience, hurling abuse at him, but as it grew more troublesome it was developing a personality uncannily like his brother's in his more disagreeable moods. It even looked like Luke. He began thinking of it as Lucas.

You ought to be ashamed of yourself, it informed him sharply.

'It's just a joke that got a little out of hand. I'll tell her the truth when the moment's right—say, about the second glass of champagne. Now shut up!'

As he emerged he found Olympia looking worried.

'Are you sure you're all right to drive?' she asked. 'Why not call the hire company from here?'

'No need. I'll see you tonight, wearing my glad rags. Goodbye for now.'

To his relief the car's damage was no more than an ugly dent, and it still moved well enough for him to get back to the hotel.

Lucas howled at him all the way.

This isn't the way to behave. What would Mamma say?

She's always telling me I should do something stupid. Well, I'm doing it. And how!

*   *   *

He'd said 'glad rags' so Olympia chose a floor-length velvet dress in dark green with a tight waist, clinging hips and a dramatic neckline. Her necklace and earrings were gold, and dainty high-heeled sandals gleamed on her feet.

She'd bought the whole outfit in anticipation of some future celebration—promotion?—but tonight was the start of a new life, and it would do fine.

She spent a long time getting her hair right. She didn't want to be the stern Miss Lincoln tonight. In the end she drew it back more loosely than usual, then twined it into long braids that she wound around her head, giving a softened effect.

When he arrived his eyes flickered over her just enough to be subtle and flattering. He said nothing, but he smiled.

She allowed her own eyes to do the same. In his bow-tie and dinner jacket he was more handsome than he had any right to be.

Downstairs he handed her gracefully into a new car.

'The hire firm actually let you have another?' she asked in disbelief.

'I talked them round. What about your garage?'

'The damage isn't too bad. I told them to send the bill to me, as we agreed.'

'Fine. I'll transfer the money into your bank on Monday morning.'

'No need. Just give me a cheque.'

He murmured something non-committal and slid away from the subject. It was dawning on him that he wasn't cut out for a double life. There was so much to remember. He would get her bank details from the firm and deposit the amount in cash so that he wouldn't have to give a name. Tonight he could have taken her to dine at the hotel where he was staying, but they knew him as Primo Rinucci, so that was out. When the bill for dinner came he would pay it in cash and brave the puzzled stares.

And in future he would 'go straight'. It was less tiring.

They swept into the Atelli, arm in arm, and were ushered to their table. It was good to be treated like a queen, she thought. This man knew how to entertain a woman and make her feel valued.

It flitted briefly across her mind that if only he were Primo Rinucci, how perfect everything would be. But she shut off the thought. That way lay weakness. Tonight was 'time out' with a delightful acquaintance. No more than that.

When the wine had been poured and the caviare served he raised his glass to her and she raised hers back.

'To a great evening and no strings,' he said.

Such an unnerving echo of her own thoughts gave her a jolt.

'No strings,' she said slowly.

'We're going to enjoy ourselves, and to blazes with the rest of them.'

'Absolutely,' she said.

Solemnly they chinked glasses.

Over caviare, she asked, 'What part of the country do you come from?'

'North London. I'll probably go back there for a visit. My father's dead but some of his relatives still live there.'

'How come you live in Italy?'

'I go back and forth. I have some Italian family and I'm just as much at home in either country, although Italy's warmer, especially Naples.'

'Naples,' she said, relishing the word. 'I've always liked the sound of it. It conjures up such pictures.'

'Urchins and cobbled streets?' he teased. 'Don't tell me you've fallen for the romantic myth?'

'Certainly not,' she said quickly. 'Myths merely get in the way of reality.'

'Maybe one can have too much reality,' he suggested.

But she shook her head decidedly.

'No. Reality is what counts.'

Once he would have said the same, but now reality was seeming less important by the minute. What mattered were the spells being woven in the air about them. And what was reality, anyway?

'I expect you'll see Naples soon enough,' he said.

'I wish I could.' She sighed.

'If you want to get anywhere in the firm, you need to be familiar with everything. Perhaps you should start learning Italian.'

'What do you mean, start?' she demanded, offended.

'Beg pardon, ma'am. How advanced are you?'

She responded with a flood of Italian words, not all of which were accurate, but it was still a pretty good effort. He was impressed.

'How was I?' she asked.

'Not bad at all. You've been working hard.'

'You bet I have! Not just since I knew about the takeover, but before that, since the first deal. I knew your firm was going to be important to us, and I wanted it to be me that did the wheeling and dealing.'

He was amazed at the intensity in her voice and the flashing of her eyes. Here was no ordinary ambition. There was a driven quality to her.

'Leonate had better look out,' he said. 'Before they know it you'll have taken over. Perhaps I should warn them.'

'No need. I can make my point for myself.'

'I'll bet you can,' he said with a touch of admiration. 'The question is, would they be wise to take you on?'

She laughed, but then sighed.

'It's easy to talk, but I thought the prize was within my grasp this time, and look what happened.'

'Curtis?' He shrugged. 'A minor prize. But now there are others, bigger, more glittering.'

'Exactly,' she said, brightening again. 'It's just a question of making the right moves and convincing the right man.'

'And who is the right man?'

She took a deep breath. Her eyes were gleaming with the thrill of the chase.

'Primo Rinucci,' she said.

He stared, jolted out of the happy dream that had begun to swirl around him.

'Who?'

'Primo Rinucci. He's the power in Leonate Europa, even I know that.'

'Yes, but—you hate him.'

'How can I when I don't know him?'

'Well, you sure gave a good imitation of it yesterday. ''To hell with Primo Rinucci'' was the kindest thing you said.'

She made an impatient gesture as if to say this was an irrelevance.

'That was just talk. Now it's time for serious business.'

'And he comes under the heading of serious business, does he?'

'Winning him over does, although it's going to be harder than I thought, since he isn't here.'

'That would make it more difficult,' he agreed solemnly.

'I suppose he didn't bother to come to England himself because we're not big enough to take up his attention.'

'You're not doing very much for my ego,' he complained.

'I didn't mean—'

'Of course you did. Be brave. Admit it. You reckon Signor Rinucci hasn't got time to inspect his English acquisition, so he sends the small fry, like me.'

'Not at all,' she said quickly. 'He sent you because you're an Englishman and therefore better able to understand what you find here.'

'Thank you, ma'am. That was a very clever recovery. You don't mean a word of it, of course, because if you thought I mattered a bean you'd be trying to impress me instead of waiting for my boss.'

She laughed and didn't deny it.

'I wouldn't get far trying to impress you now, would I?' she teased. 'It's too late. You already know the worst of me. But he doesn't.'

She looked at him in sudden anxiety. 'You won't tell him, will you?'

'What, that you abused him?'

'No, that I'm lying in wait for him. I don't want him to be one step ahead of me, always knowing what I'm doing, do I?'

'No, you don't want that,' he agreed awkwardly.

'So you won't tell him about me?'

'Not unless he asks me direct questions,' he said 'which I'm sure he won't.'

'Good. Then I'm going to lure the lion into my den.'

He grinned. 'I guess I don't qualify as a lion.'

'I see you more as a bear,' she agreed, giving the matter serious thought. 'Brown and grizzly, with a growl that you have to listen to very carefully to work out what it means today. Is he ferocious or is he in a mood to have his fur stroked? Better get it right, or who knows what could happen?'

It was subtle. It was clever. It was beautifully calculated to butter him up and soothe him down and, heaven help him, he knew he was going to fall for it even while he could see her pulling the strings.

'Congratulations!' he said admiringly. 'At least I've had my warning. You'll use me for practice, until the real prey turns up.'

She turned on him, eyes shining gleefully, head on one side.

'You don't mind, do you?'

'How kind of you to ask! Would it make any difference if I did?'

'You could always refuse.'

Sure, he could refuse! Like a drowning man could refuse to go down for the third time!

He met her eyes.

'I'm considering my options,' he said. 'But have you thought of the practical difficulties?'

'How do you mean?'

'Aren't you going to find it a little hard, running a lion and a bear in tandem?'

'Ah, but suppose the bear's on my side and he's helping me, discreetly of course?'

'Helping you—how?' he asked, with well-founded caution.

'Inside information. Practical advice. We could be a great team.'

'A team implies an equal bargain,' he protested. 'Advantage on both sides. What do I get out of it?'

'What do you want to get out of it?' she teased.

Suddenly his head swam. What did he want to get out of it?

When the wild dance of his senses had calmed a little he managed to speak.

'If that means what I think it does,' he said softly, 'you're a shameless hussy.'

'Not at all. You know the score.'

'Maybe I have my own method of scoring.'

'That will only make it more interesting,' she murmured, so softly that he had to strain to hear, and her breath whispered across his face.

Out of sight, he gripped the table.

'You're a wicked woman,' he said appreciatively. 'Scheming, manipulative, dishonest—'

'No.' She laid a finger over his lips. 'I'm not dishonest. I'm completely upfront about what I want and what I'll do to get it. That's honest. It doesn't make me a very nice person, but it does make me honest.'

'Olympia, for heaven's sake! What a way to talk! Anyway, what do you mean by "inside information"?'

'What's the best way to approach him? What kind of woman does he like?'

'The kind he's married to,' he replied, straight-faced.

Her eyes opened wide. *'He's married?'*

'Suffocatingly married for the last twelve years. He has five children and his wife's a dragon with gimlet eyes. She's a jealous fiend who inspects all his female employees with a machine-gun in her hand.'

'But Cedric says—' She checked herself, finally seeing the glint in his eyes. She leaned back in her chair, glaring at him.

'I ought to squirt something at you for scaring me like that.'

'It's all true, I swear it.'

'True, nothing! He's a bachelor. Cedric told me.'

'So you've been pumping poor Cedric?' he exclaimed in unholy delight. 'I can't wait to hear what you offered *him.*'

Suddenly she could no longer meet his eyes. 'The usual,' she murmured.

'And just—what—is the usual?' he asked, smothering his unease.

'Well—you know—'

'Tell me.'

'Whatever his heart desires. It has to be that, or there's no point.'

He drew a long, painful breath. If she didn't answer soon, so help him, he was on the point of violence.

'And what did Cedric's heart desire?' he asked with a deadly smile.

Olympia looked around in both directions before replying in a low voice. 'Cedric has a *particular interest.* He doesn't talk a lot about it because—well, people are so quick to make judgements—'

'But he knew you'd understand?' Primo said grimly.

'Oh, yes. He's shown me his whole collection, and I was able to complete it. He was really pleased.'

'Complete it?'

'Yes, he collects videos about dinosaurs, and there was one he'd never been able to get hold of. Luckily my father had it, so I copied it for him. Cedric eats out of my hand now.'

He stared at her. 'Dinosaurs,' he said, dazed.

'Yes.'

'You got him a video about dinosaurs?' he repeated slowly.

'That was what his heart desired.'

Her eyes were full of fun, telling him he'd been well and truly had. He tried to quell his laughter but it welled up inside him, finally bursting out loud enough to startle a passing waiter.

'You tricky, devious—' he choked.

'But whatever did you think I meant?' she asked, wide-eyed and innocent.

'I daren't tell you. You'd probably slap my face.'

Of course she'd followed his every thought, because she was a black-haired witch who could tease a man into her glittering snares, even when he knew he ought to run a mile. That was the sensible thing to do.

But he'd been sensible all his life, and suddenly it was impossible.

CHAPTER FOUR

IT TOOK him a while to stop choking with laughter and sit shaking his head as he regarded her in delight.

'You should be ashamed of yourself,' she said sternly.

'So should you,' he riposted at once. 'Now tell me, was Cedric's information worth the price?'

'No, I'm afraid Cedric's knowledge is limited. He couldn't even say what Signor Rinucci looked like, although he's met him. ''Tallish'', is the best he could do.'

'Yes, I don't think noticing details is poor Cedric's strong suit.'

'But you'll know. Is he good-looking? What sort of things does he enjoy? Come on. Tell.'

'Are you planning to seduce him?' he asked, avoiding her eyes.

'Certainly not. I'll be far more subtle than that. Seduction merely complicates things.

Besides, when you say seduction, what exactly do you mean?'

'I'm disappointed in you, Olympia. I thought you were a strong woman, not one who backed away from facts. You know exactly what seduction means. The whole thing. Admit it. You haven't thought this through.'

'Not thought it through? If you knew just how many hours, waking and sleeping, I've spent working out this—'

'But you've never gone as far as the logical conclusion.'

'Look, there's seduction and there's seduction—'

'No, there isn't. There's only seduction, and you'd better know what you mean by it before you set out after this man. He'll want far more than a dinosaur video. Just how far are you prepared to go?'

'Not that far. What do you take me for?'

'A woman prepared to put her ambition before everything else. Before love, before happiness, before being a person.'

'That depends on what you mean by being a person. To me it means being a success. I want to impress him with my knowledge of business, my ability to speak his language, my willingness to commit myself to the job one hundred per cent.'

'And you're not going to use your womanly wiles at all? Is that it?'

She shrugged lightly. 'I may not be the kind of woman he likes.'

'Oh, he likes them all,' Primo said, throwing caution to the winds. 'He's dangerous.'

'Dangerous, how?' she asked eagerly.

He racked his brain, searching for ways to describe his 'other' self. He was beginning to find this exhilarating.

'He's a womaniser,' he said recklessly, 'a man without discrimination. If you've got any sense, you won't tangle with him.'

'Oh, but I love a challenge.'

'But he won't be a challenge. It's too easy to attract him on that level, but what happens afterwards?'

'Then I'll move on to Plan B.'

'You've got it all worked out,' he observed wryly.

'You have to work things out to get what you want.'

'And Primo Rinucci is what you want?'

'Not him personally. What I want is his power and influence.'

'And his money?'

'Not at all,' she said, shocked. 'Just his power. I can make my own money.'

'I just can't work you out.'

'Excellent. Then I'm on the right track. He mustn't be able to work me out either.'

'Can we forget Rinucci?' he said, a tad edgily. 'There are some holes in your reasoning that you'll have to consider later, but I'd prefer not to spend this evening on the subject.'

'What?' she said at once. 'What holes?'

He sighed and gave in. 'Well, for a start, there's the troop of lovers that you seem to keep dancing after you. Won't they get in the way rather?'

'What troop of lovers? I don't have any lovers. At least—' She seemed to consider. 'No,' she said at last. 'Not at the moment.'

'Admirers then. All those cards this morning, two without a message and one that said, *"I'll never forget"*. Who is he, and what won't he forget?'

'Ah, that was from Brendan,' she said with a smile. 'We had a flirtation a few years back and I get a card every year.'

'A flirtation, was it?' he couldn't resist saying.

'Brendan's a great one for pretty gestures at a safe distance. He always makes sure he's on the other side of the world in February. This came from Australia.'

'And the other two? And the red roses?'

Suddenly she burst out laughing, not a soft teasing sound but a chuckle of genuine mirth.

'You won't believe me when I tell you.'

'Try me.'

'They were from my parents.'

'*"To the one and only, the girl who transformed the world",*' he quoted.

'They'd been married twenty years before I came along, and they'd given up hope. As long as I can remember they've sent me Valentine cards and flowers with messages about how I changed the world for them. They're such darlings.'

'Well, I'll be—is that for real?'

'Yes, I swear it's the truth. Didn't you see their picture on the bookcase?'

'Yes, but I thought they must be your grandparents.'

'That's because they're both nearly seventy.'

'But why didn't you tell me this morning?'

'Because I was enjoying myself. I don't mind being thought of as a woman with a host of admirers.'

'Miss Lincoln, you have the soul of a tease.'

'Sure I have. It's very useful. My husband got quite uptight about those cards at first. Right to the end I'm not sure he really believed my parents sent them.'

'The end? You're a widow?'

'Oh, no, he's still alive. He came close to meeting a sudden end a few times but I resisted that temptation.'

'Your better self asserted itself.'

'No, I don't have a better self,' she said cheerfully. 'He just wasn't worth the hassle. With my luck, I'd never have got away with it, so I let him live.'

She finished with a shrug, as though the whole thing was just too trivial for words, but he felt as though he'd had a glimpse through a keyhole. It was narrow, but the details he could see suggested a whole vista, waiting to be revealed.

The waiter appeared to clear away their plates.

'I gather he didn't deserve to live,' Primo said casually.

'That's what I thought, but I'm probably doing him an injustice. He wasn't really the monster I made him into. I told myself that love conquered all, and then blamed him when that turned out to be nonsense. And we married too young. I was eighteen, he was twenty-one. I suppose we changed into different people—or discovered the people we really were all the time.'

'I don't think this is who you really were all the time,' he said with sudden urgency. 'This is what he did to you.'

'He taught me a lot of things, including the value of total and utter selfishness. Boy, is that ever the way to get ahead! Tunnel vision. Wear blinkers and look straight down the line to what you want.'

He'd often said the same himself, but he couldn't bear hearing his own ruthlessness from her.

'Don't,' he said, reaching out swiftly and laying a finger over her lips. 'Don't talk like that.'

'You're right,' she said, moving her lips against his finger before he drew it away. 'It's too revealing, isn't it? I need a better act. How lucky that I have you to practise on.'

'Yes, isn't it?' he said wryly.

'I mean that I don't have to pretend with you. We can afford honesty. Why, what is it?' She'd seen his sudden unease.

'Nothing,' he said quickly. 'But the waiter wants to serve the next course.'

The mention of honesty had reminded him that he was sailing under false colours. But at the same time he had an exhilarating feeling of having found a new kind of honesty. His heart was open to her, his defences down as never before. Was this what Hope had been trying to tell him all the time?

'So your husband taught you all about self-ishness?' he said.

'I guess I was a willing learner.'

It hurt him to hear her slander herself, but she seemed driven to do it, as though that way she could erect a defensive shield against the world.

'Did you ever want children?'

She hesitated a long time before saying, 'I wanted *his* children. I hadn't thought of myself as the maternal type at first. It was going to be a career for me, although I thought I'd probably want children later. Then I'd find a way to juggle them both.'

'So the career wasn't going to be everything to you?' he asked cautiously. 'Not like now.'

'No, not like now. But then I met David and it overturned all my ideas. I wanted to be his wife and have his babies so much that it hurt.

'Somehow it was never the right time for him. He said we were too young—which I suppose we were, and there were ''things to do first''. That's how he put it. I just said yes to whatever he wanted. It seemed a fair bargain as long as he loved me.'

She said the words with no deliberate attempt at pathos, but with a kind of incredulous wonder that anyone could believe such stuff.

'But he didn't,' Primo said gently.

She made no reply. She was barely conscious of him. Something had drawn her back into the person she used to be, naïve, giving and totally, blindly in love. The impression was so strong that she could almost feel David there again—confident, charming, with the ability to take her to the top of the world— then dash her down.

Never again.

'No, he didn't,' she said. 'I was useful to him, but only for a while. He used to wear expensive clothes because he had to make a good impression at work. I made do with the cheapest I could find because who cared what I looked like?'

'Didn't he?'

'You should have heard him on that subject. He was very good. ''Darling, it doesn't matter whether your dress is costly or the cheapest thing in the market. To me, you're always beautiful.'' What is it?'

She asked the question because he had covered his eyes in anguish.

'I can't bear this,' he said. 'It's such a corny line. I thought it was dead and buried years ago.'

'Well, it rose from the grave,' she said tartly. 'And, to save you asking, yes, I fell for it. Hook, line and sinker.'

'I'll bet *he* wasn't wearing the cheapest thing on the market.'

'You're right. I bought him a shirt once—not expensive, but I thought it was nice. He sat me down, explained that he couldn't be seen in it, and asked if I had the receipt. He returned it to the shop, got the money back, then added some money of his own to buy what he called "a decent one". It was his way of letting me know what was good enough for him and what wasn't.'

'And you let him live?' Primo demanded, scandalised.

'I think I was kind of hypnotised by him. I wouldn't let myself believe what I was discovering. And he looked fantastic in the new shirt. If a man's incredibly handsome you somehow don't think he can be a jerk.'

She lapsed into silence and sat brooding into her glass, trying to make a difficult decision. What came next was something she'd never been able to speak of before.

Yet here she was, on the verge of telling her most painful secret to a man she'd known only a day. But that day might have been a year, she seemed to know him so well. All her instincts reassured her that he was a friend and she could trust him with anything.

'Tell me,' he said gently. 'What happened then?'

She gave a faint smile.

'He had to work on a marketing project. By that time I had a job in the same firm. I was down at the bottom of the ladder but I understood the business and I helped him with the project. I'd done that before and, if I say it myself, the best ideas in that project were mine.

'In fact the layout and presentation were mine too. He used to say that my talent was knowing how to say things. I was flattered, until it dawned on me that what he really meant was that he was the one with talent, and all I could do was the superficial stuff.'

'But firms will pay big money for someone who can do "the superficial stuff". It's what marketing and presentation is about, and I'm surprised you don't know that.'

She gave him a shy smile that went to his heart.

'Well, I do know it now,' she said. 'But not then. I didn't understand a lot of things then. As far as I knew, David was the great talent in the family.'

'Because that's what he kept telling you?'

'Yes.'

'Meanwhile he stole your ideas and used them to climb the ladder?'

'He was promoted to be the boss's deputy. That's how he met the boss's daughter, who was also working there. One day I went up to the top floor to pay him a surprise visit. We'd had a row and I wanted to make up. Rosalie was there, leaning forward over his desk, with her head close to his.

'She scowled and demanded to know who I was, looking down her nose at me. I told her I was David's wife and she gasped. He hadn't told her he was married. Nobody in the firm knew. Our surname was Smith, which is so common that nobody made the connection.

'That night he came home late. I spent the time crying, like the wimp I was. When he got home we had a big fight. I said how dare he pretend I didn't exist, and he looked me up and down and said, "Why would I want to tell anyone about you?"'

'*Bastardo!*'

'I had nothing to say. She was so beautiful and perfectly groomed, and I was so dowdy.

Soon after that we split up. There was a divorce and he married Rosalie. Since then he's gone right to the top.'

'Of course,' he said cynically. 'The boss's son-in-law always goes to the top.'

She nodded. 'His father-in-law is a rich man with a lot of power.' She gave a curt laugh. 'David has two children now. A friend of mine has seen them. She says they're beautiful.'

'And they should have been yours,' he said gently.

She was suddenly unable to speak. But then she recovered and said, 'No, of course not. That's just being sentimental. When the divorce came through I did a lot more crying, so much that I reckon I've used up all my tears for the rest of my life. That's what I promised myself, anyway. That was when I resumed my maiden name.

'It's silly to brood about the past. You can't rewrite it. You can only make sure that the future is better. And that's what I'm determined to do.'

Primo didn't know what to say. She seemed to speak lightly but her manner was still charged with emotion. What unsettled him most was the way she'd revealed her pain with the sudden force of someone breaking boundaries for the first time. Now she seemed to be withdrawing back into herself, as if regretting the brief intimacy she'd permitted.

She confirmed it when she laughed and said, 'And that's the story of my life.'

'No, not your life, just one bad experience. But don't judge all men by your husband. Some of us have redeeming qualities.'

'Of course. I like men. I enjoy their company. But I'm always waiting for that moment when the true face shows through.'

'But suppose you saw the true face at the start,' he suggested, fencing, hoping to draw her out further.

'Does any man show his true face at the start?' she fenced back. 'Did you, for instance?'

'Yes, let's forget about that,' he said hastily. 'I prefer to talk some more about you.'

'Why? Is the truth about you so very terrible?'

He was wildly tempted to say that the truth about himself was something she wouldn't believe. But he recovered his sanity in time.

'Tell me about the new Olympia, the one who knows that love is nonsense.'

'At least she knows it's something you have to be realistic about.'

'I think you could lose a lot by being that sort of realist.'

'But don't you believe a person's head should rule their heart, and they should avoid stupid risks?'

'No, I don't,' he said, aghast. 'You could hardly say anything worse about any man.'

'Not at all. They're admirable qualities.'

'Yes, for a dummy in a shop window.'

'Have I offended you?'

'Yes,' he growled.

'But why? Most men like to be admired for their brains and common sense.'

He recovered his good humour.

'You've observed that, have you? Is it on your list of effective techniques for use against Rinucci? Item one, sub-section A. Make breathless comments about size of brain and staggering use thereof. Note: Try to sound convincing, however difficult. Sub-section B. Suggest that—'

'Stop it,' she said, laughing. 'Anyway, I don't know if it would work with him. Is he intelligent enough to make admiration of his brains convincing?'

'It doesn't matter. If he isn't, he'll never know the difference.'

'That's true,' she said, much struck.

'Personally I've always considered him rather a stupid man.'

'Stupid in what way?' she wanted to know.

'In every way.'

'Stupid in every way,' she repeated. 'That's a start.'

Primo grinned suddenly and hailed a passing waiter.

'Would you bring the lady a notebook and pencil, please?' he asked. 'She has urgent notes to make.' Turning back to Olympia, he said, 'Of course, if you were really applying yourself to the job, you'd have brought them with you.'

'I wasn't exactly prepared for the conversation to be so promising.'

'Always be prepared. You never know where any conversation might lead—*what are you writing?*'

'Always—be—prepared—' she said, her eyes fixed on the notebook which the waiter had just placed before her. Then she raised them and fixed them admiringly on his face. 'How clever you are! I'd never have thought of a difficult concept like that for myself.'

'Behave yourself,' he said in a voice that shook with laughter.

'But I was admiring your brilliant advice.'

'You were using me for target practice.'

'Well, some targets are more fun to practise on than others.'

The significant chuckle in her voice was almost his undoing. He longed to ask her to expand on the subject, but he felt she'd had it all her own way long enough.

'Enough,' he said severely. 'If you're going to do this, do it properly. Don't be obvious. Even a fool like Rinucci could see through that.'

'Really? Never mind, you can tell me what else to say. How old is he?'

'About my age.'

'That's young to be in his position.'

'He relies a lot on family influence,' Primo said, ruthlessly sacrificing his own reputation.

'It's going to take a lot of work filling this notebook. I'll need a section for his interests, clothes—'

'He's a fancy dresser. More money than sense. Ah, but I forgot. You're not interested in his money.'

'That's right. I just want to run him to earth, rope and brand him—'

'And generally get him in a state of total subjection.'

'You got it. And then—'

'Olympia, could we possibly drop the subject of Primo Rinucci?' he asked plaintively. 'He really isn't a very interesting man.'

'I'm sorry. Of course he isn't interesting to you.'

The waiter, proffering the sweet menu, saved him from having to answer, and after that he managed to divert her on to another subject.

At last she said, 'Maybe we should go. I should go to work tomorrow, to impress the boss.'

'But it is Sunday and he isn't here.'

'I meant you.'

'Yes, right—I'm getting confused. Let's go.'

On the way home they talked in a relaxed, disjointed way, then made the last part of the journey in silence. When he drew up and looked over to her he saw that she was asleep.

Her breathing was so soft that he could hardly hear it. She slept like a contented child, her face softened, all the tension smoothed out. There was even a faint smile on her lips, as though she'd found a rare moment of contentment.

He moved closer, charmed by the way her long black lashes lay against her cheek. If this had been any other woman, on any other night, he would have leaned down and laid his mouth against hers, teasing gently until she awoke and her lips parted under his. Then he would have taken her into his arms, letting her head rest against his shoulder and her hair spread out, flowing over his arm.

They would have held each other for a long moment before he finally murmured a question and she whispered her assent. Then, perhaps, they would have made their way together up to her apartment and closed the door behind them.

So many evenings had ended that way, in tenderness, pleasure and passion. But not with her.

With this woman passion was forbidden. Only tenderness was allowed, and so he watched her silently for several minutes, holding her hand but making no other move, until she opened her eyes and he said, in a shaking voice, 'I think you should go upstairs now. You won't mind if I don't escort you to your door, will you?'

He watched her walk into the building and kept his eyes on the windows he knew were hers until he saw the lights go on. Then he drove away quickly while he was still safe.

CHAPTER FIVE

As DAWN broke Olympia became half awake, seeming to exist in a limbo where there were no facts, only feelings and misty uncertainties, but they were very sweet. Perhaps more sweet for being undefined.

She seemed to be back in his car, dozing as they made the journey home. She couldn't see or hear him, but she was intensely aware of him. When he took her hand in his she was pervaded by a sense of deep contentment, as though she had come home to a place of safety, where lived the only person who understood.

She was smiling as she opened her eyes.

For once, the hours ahead of her were unknown, the decisions in the hand of someone else. After only two days he already seemed to fill her world. She was looking forward to the moment when she would meet him today and see in his eyes that he remembered last night, how they'd laughed and gazed into each other's minds and recognised what they found there.

When the phone rang she snatched it up eagerly.

'Olympia?'

'Jack? I knew it would be you.'

'Why? Did the ring sound impatient?'

She laughed, feeling excited. He was impatient to see her. He'd called to suggest a meeting today.

'Well, yes,' she said. 'It did sound a little impatient.'

'That's because I'm going through books and realising how much there is to do. If I spend the rest of the day working I'll just be ready to leave tomorrow. It ought to be today, of course, but since it's Sunday it'll have to wait.'

'Did you say you were leaving?' she asked, in shock, as much because of his businesslike tone as his words.

'I need to see the rest of the Curtis empire.'

'Empire? You mean the two other tiny factories?'

'That's right. I've studied them on-line and through correspondence. Now I want you to show them to me. Pack clothes for several days away, and I'll collect you first thing tomorrow. Bye for now.'

He hung up without further discussion, leaving her wondering if he was the same man as the night before.

The impression was reinforced when they met the next day. He was pleasant but impersonal. The evening they had spent together might never have happened.

Hadson's, the first factory, was in the south. As he drove they discussed business, how this small, out of the way place had come to be acquired, the computer peripherals that it made, how economic was it. Olympia spoke carefully, unwilling to be the one who revealed the awkward truth about Hadson's, which was that it was too small to survive. He would see it soon enough.

'You've gone very quiet,' he said at last.

'I've given you the facts and figures, but you need to form your own impression.'

To her relief he didn't press her further.

'Shall I call to say we're coming?'

'No, it's better to take them by surprise,' he replied coolly.

In another hour they reached the little village of Andelwick and went to the factory, where the surprise was very obvious. So was the alarm, almost fear. Introducing the forty staff, Olympia praised every one of them individually, trying to keep a pleading note out of her voice. Sounding desperate would not help them.

He was charming to everyone and invited the three senior staff to lunch. There he drew facts and figures out of them with skill and so much subtlety that they might not have guessed what lay behind it. But they did, Olympia realised with a sinking heart. They already knew the worst.

When they were alone he looked at her and said, 'Hmm!'

'Don't you dare say "Hmm!" to me,' she exploded. 'I know what you're thinking.'

'I'm thinking we're going to have to stay overnight. Is there a good hotel?'

'No hotels in this tiny place, but The Rising Sun does rooms. It's a nice pub, basic but clean, and the food's great. It's just down the road.'

'Fine. Will you go there now and do the bookings? Oh—and—' he was suddenly awkward '—I seem to have left my credit cards behind. Could you use yours?'

'Sure, no problem.'

He spent the afternoon studying the books, said 'Hmm!' again, and swept her off to The Rising Sun, an old, traditional building where she'd booked two tiny rooms with such low oak beams that it was hard to walk upright.

As she'd promised, the food was excellent and gave them vigour for the fight.

'You can't just dump this place,' she said fiercely.

'It's not viable, Olympia. You can see that for yourself. Forty employees!'

'Who all work their socks off for you.'

'They're now part of an international conglomerate—'

'So loyalty doesn't matter any more?'

'Will you let me get a word in edgeways? It might have been viable until two years ago, but now there's that other place, just down the road, Kellway's—who are operating in much the same line of work.'

'The council should never have allowed them to start up. They're just trying to squeeze us out of business.'

'Us?'

'Hadson's. It's just a unit of productivity to you, isn't it?'

'It's my job to see things in that way.'

'And to hell with the people! But Mr Jakes is a sweet old man and he's been the backbone of this place for years.'

'Perhaps he's ready to put his feet up?'

'No way, he loves that job and he wants to stick with it. And what about Jenny? It's her first job and she's so keen.'

'Yes, but—'

'And jobs are very hard to come by in this area. Did you know that? No, of course you didn't. All you care about is books of figures and money.'

'That's all I'm supposed to care about. And so are you.'

She missed the warning, yielding to the anger that was carrying her along.

'They're people, not just statistics.'

'This is business.'

'To hell with business!'

Silence.

He was regarding her wryly.

'If Primo Rinucci heard you say that, you'd be dead,' he observed.

Aghast, she saw the trap she'd created for herself.

'But he didn't hear me,' she said. 'Only you.'

'Only me,' he agreed with an odd inflection in his voice that she couldn't quite understand. 'I won't tell him, but sooner or later the truth will out.'

'What truth?' she asked in a hollow voice.

'That underneath that calculating, hard-as-nails exterior you've so carefully painted on there's a soft-hearted, empathetic, generous human being.'

'It's a lie,' she said fiercely.

He grinned and took a swig of the local beer before asking, 'Where did you get all that detailed knowledge of Hadson's?'

'I spent a week there once.'

'And got to know them all as people?'

'I did a detailed survey of the situation, as my job required,' she said stiffly.

'And made friends with them,' he persisted remorselessly. 'Liked them, felt for them.'

'I suppose one can be a human being without becoming an automaton.'

'Not really. Sooner or later the choice has to be made. My dear girl—'

'Don't call me that. I'm not a girl, I'm not yours and I'm not dear to you.'

'Isn't that for me to say?' he asked quietly.

She was silent a moment before saying, equally quietly, 'That's enough!'

He shrugged. 'Whatever pleases you. It's time I went to my room and spent some more time in the soulless pursuit of money. Goodnight.'

He left her there, wondering how she could ever have thought he was a nice guy. He was a monster who called her vile, unspeakable names.

Soft-hearted. Empathetic. *Generous* for Pete's sake!

She would never forgive him!

The following morning she rose to find that he had compounded his crimes. There was no sign of him at breakfast, only a note.

I'm tied up this morning, but I'll join you at Hadson's later. JC

Brusque to the point of discourtesy, she fumed. Perhaps he found writing difficult. He certainly seemed to have had a problem at the end of the note because there was an inky smudge just before his initials, as though he'd started to write something else, then scrubbed it out. Maybe he didn't know his own initials, she thought uncharitably.

Her morning at Hadson's wasn't happy. They all suspected the worst, and she could only confirm it.

'He says the place isn't viable,' she said with a sigh. 'It's just a matter of time now. I'm so sorry.'

'We know you did your best,' Mr Jakes told her and the others murmured agreement.

She was left feeling cast down. She had mishandled the whole business, failed to save their jobs and they were being nice to her. She could have wept.

He turned up in the middle of the afternoon and was received in near silence.

'Sorry to keep you waiting, everyone,' he said, apparently oblivious to the atmosphere.

'This morning's business took longer than I expected, owing to Mr Kellway's difficulty in making up his mind. But in the end he saw things the right way.'

'You've been to Kellway's?' Olympia asked, astounded.

'I've bought it. There's no room for both of you, so there'll be a merger. Those who want to continue working are guaranteed a job at Kellway's. Those who don't can apply for voluntary redundancy.'

Forty faces turned accusingly towards Olympia.

'But she said you were going to close us down and chuck us out,' Mr Jakes said.

'Did you say that?' Jack Cayman asked.

'I—not in those exact words. But you said—'

'I said this place wasn't viable, and it isn't, on its own. A merger makes sense. I never mentioned chucking people out. That was your spin. You shouldn't jump to conclusions.'

'I—'

'Before we leave we'd better sort out who wants to stay and who doesn't. Mr Jakes, your position is protected. Kellway's is eager to get you.'

'You mean I don't get the redundancy?' Mr Jakes demanded.

'Of course, if you want it.'

'You bet I want it. I can go and see my daughter in Australia.'

Olympia stared. Was there anything she hadn't got wrong?

It took a couple of hours before they were ready to leave and then the cheers followed them. As they walked back to the pub he said, 'Do we have time to reach the other place to-night?'

'Just about.'

She took the wheel for the three hour drive. They said little on the journey, each saving energy for what was to come. This time the journey was to the Midlands and they managed to find a small hotel, just in time for the last serving of dinner.

Only when they were sitting over the soup did she say crossly, 'You made a complete fool of me.'

'I didn't mean to. You shouldn't have made that announcement without consulting me first.'

'I never thought you'd do anything like that. Anyway, suppose Signor Rinucci doesn't agree with you about this purchase?'

'He will.'

'Just like that?'

'Why not? It's the logical next step. You didn't see it because you haven't the right mindset, but you'll learn.'

'The right mindset for Leonate, you mean?'

'No, for any successful business. You're still thinking on a small scale and that's no use for an international conglomerate.'

'So how do I learn to think ''international'' if I can't get to meet the big boss?'

'Still fixated on him, huh?'

'You knew that.'

'Nothing's changed?'

'Nothing,' she said firmly.

'What about all that warmth and humanity you were showing signs of?'

'An aberration. I'll get over it. Besides, look what a mess I made. I got Mr Jakes all wrong. But you didn't,' she added as the realisation came to her. 'You understood him.'

'So maybe I'm not just figures and accounts?' he said with a slight inflection of teasing.

'Did I say that? I don't remember.'

'You're tired. That was a long drive and we have a lot to get through tomorrow. Let's finish the meal and get some rest.'

She was only too glad to agree. She felt as though something had knocked her sideways, but she couldn't quite work out what it was.

Tired as she was, she found it hard to sleep. Lying awake for hours, she became aware of him on the other side of the thin wall. She could hear his bed creak, his footsteps on the floor, his window being pushed up as if he were drinking in the night air, then his bed again, sounding as though he were tossing and turning.

She wondered what he was thinking and why he should be as restless as herself.

The next day was more successful. As before, they arrived without warning and walked in as the manager was talking with a dissatisfied customer. It soon became clear that a trivial matter had been blown out of all proportion, chiefly because the customer had a quarrelsome nature.

He was inclined to take umbrage at the new arrivals, but within minutes Olympia had taken over, dazzled the man with her smile and calmed him down to the point where a sensible conversation became possible.

By the time she had finished, the order was not only rescued but increased and the customer was purring with content. Primo took them all to lunch and kept the manager locked in conversation while Olympia completed her demolition job on the customer.

They left town in time to get back to London quite early and laughed all the way.

'You did a great job,' he told her. 'I've never seen a fish reeled in so cleverly. How about we celebrate tonight?'

Her answer was a blissful sigh.

In mid-afternoon he dropped her at her apartment block.

'We'll go to The Diamond Parrot,' he said, naming London's newest and plushest night-club. 'Do you have a black dress?'

'I think so,' she said cautiously, knowing that she hadn't.

'Well, you'd better take the rest of the afternoon off to make sure,' he said, understanding perfectly.

He might have meant any kind of black dress, but the one she purchased was definitely slinky. It was made from silk and hugged her hips in a satisfactory way. When he saw it he gave a nod of satisfaction.

'That's just how I imagined you when I bought this,' he said, producing a black velvet box.

Inside was a delicate set of diamond earrings and matching pendant.

'A bonus for a job well done,' he said.

'From the firm?'

'Certainly from the firm. We cherish our valuable employees.'

He watched as she slipped the earrings into place, then turned so that he could drape the pendant around her neck. To his dismay he discovered that he was reluctant. Her long neck was white and perfect, an invitation that he must not accept. He tried to fasten the clasp without touching her, then backed off quickly, lest he yield to the temptation to drop a kiss on her nape.

'Fine, let's go,' he said in a voice that he hoped didn't shake.

She looked around with a little frown, as though in surprise. He turned away from that surprise, afraid of the insight it might create. She must never guess, not until he was ready to tell her, and they could laugh together, sharing the moment of discovery.

That time, when it came, would be sweet. But it couldn't be rushed without risking everything.

He hadn't yet defined what 'everything' might mean, but he knew that with each word, each step he had to be more careful. If this had been a conventional relationship he would have often taken her into his arms by now, kissing her long and fervently, letting passion take them wherever it might. But that was forbidden while she didn't know the truth. Even his thoughts were forbidden, although the struggle to rein them in grew harder every moment.

It was like conducting a clandestine relationship with a married woman, he thought in frustration. Except that he, himself, was the betrayed 'husband'.

Suddenly the evening ahead didn't seem like such a good idea. She would sit beside him, beautiful, glowing, and he must try to stay calm.

He groaned.

They found The Diamond Parrot in festive mode, having decided to make St Valentine's Day last a while longer.

'St Valentine's Week,' he murmured as they entered through dark red velvet curtains. 'It's original. I wish I could say the same about the roses and the glittering hearts.'

'They've really overdone it, haven't they?' Olympia chuckled.

A waiter showed them to a table on the edge of the dance floor. One or two couples were already smooching around to the music of a small band and a glittery chanteuse who crooned about moon and June.

For a while they talked little, but relaxed after the hard work of the last two days. Olympia felt good, knowing she had impressed him, and knowing also that she looked her best. From time to time she touched the delicate diamonds about her neck, puzzled again by the constraint she had sensed in his manner as he'd clasped it about her neck.

She had waited for the feel of his fingers gently caressing the sensitive nape, as any other man would have done. But there had been nothing but the most impersonal touch as he'd fixed the clasp. She hadn't even felt his breath against her skin, as though he were standing back to avoid her.

'You shouldn't be here,' she said. 'You should be making your report to Head Office.'

'After the roller coaster of the last few days I need to think about what I'm going to say. You make it difficult because you're never the same person from one moment to the next.'

'You don't have to tell them about me as a person, just as a businesswoman.'

'As a businesswoman you're impressive. What you did with that customer today— well—'

'That's just part of my repertoire,' she said with a chuckle. 'The trick is to get his attention first with the old-fashioned fluttering eye technique. Then, when he's got you down as a stupid bimbo, you bash him over the head with facts and figures. Leaves 'em reeling every time.'

'You're good at the fluttering eye bit, I take it.'

'Yes, but if you do it slowly it's more effective.

She gave a long sigh, lowering and raising her eyelids just once, very slowly. He drew a sharp breath. It was like seeing her eyes for the first time ever, unprepared for their impact. To make it worse, she gave a languorous smile, letting her lips fall apart very slightly.

'Is that what you plan to do with him?' he asked.

'Him?' she asked vaguely. 'Who?'

'Primo Rinucci.'

She was suddenly angry. Why did he have to drag Primo Rinucci into everything?

'You think that'll work, huh?' she asked in a slightly edgy voice.

'Sure to. Especially with all the practice you're getting on me. Teasing is always a good bet, especially when you manage to keep your distance at the same time. It'll stop him getting the wrong ideas. Either that or it'll incite him to more ideas. One of the two. You'll have to decide which you want. It wouldn't do to become confused.'

'It may not give him any ideas at all,' she couldn't resist saying. 'It seems to leave you cold.'

'It isn't supposed to give me ideas,' he pointed out. 'I'm just here to help you in your mission in life. When you've sharpened your claws on me, you'll bring your lion down.'

She chuckled suddenly.

'When I've done that, will you take pictures of me standing with one foot on his helpless form, like the old hunters used to do?'

'I'll even help you mount his head on the wall,' he promised. 'You can put it in the centre of all the other trophies.'

'What other trophies?'

'The others you've used for practice, with my head in the centre.'

'Uh-uh!' she said, shaking her head. 'You can stay cool about it. That's what makes you so valuable.'

It was a let-out and he should have seized it, but some demon urged him on to say, 'I should have thought it made me useless. If nothing works with me, how are you going to know what works with him?'

'Aha!' She seemed much struck by this point of view. After considering for a moment she asked, 'Do you and he have the same tastes?'

'Pretty similar,' he said, crossing his fingers and wishing he'd never started this.

'Is he—or you—sophisticated or corny?'

'How do you mean, corny?'

'You remember those old Hollywood films where the heroine wore her hair tight back, then pulled it loose to signify that she was starting a new life? That kind of corny.'

'I don't think I ever saw those films,' he said, rashly tempting fate.

'Like this.'

With a swift movement, she tugged at her hair so that it came free, flooding over her bare shoulders like a black silky fountain. Some of it fell down the sides of her face, throwing her features into mysterious shadow.

Una strega. Una bellissima strega magica.

'That's how they do it,' she said, 'and the hero takes one look at her and goes gaga, because he's thinking, How can that grim-faced harpy have turned into this seductive creature? And she doesn't tell him the truth, which is that it took six hours and the entire make-up department, and if he's fool enough to marry her it's the grim harpy he'll find on the pillow in the morning. Oh, no, she lets him think it's the power of *ler-rrve*.'

The satirical inflection she put on the last word had him choking with laughter. At the same time, he wished she hadn't used the words 'pillow' and 'in the morning'. This was hard enough without her turning it into a testing ground for self-control.

'They tend to believe in *ler-rrve* in films,' he said. 'If they showed your point of view, nobody would go. No—leave it as it is.' She'd begun drawing her hair back again. 'Keep it like that while I do some thinking. It might give me some ideas to improve your technique.'

'I'm glad you have a sense of proportion about this,' she said. 'It's a great help. Unless—' She stopped as a horrible thought assailed her. 'Jack, you're not—? I mean, this isn't all pointless, is it? You'd have told me?'

'Told you what?'

'You know what I mean.'

'No, I don't.' In fact he did, but he'd be blowed if he'd let her off the hook that easily. Let her suffer for a change.

'You're not—are you?'

He gave her a twisted smile. 'Are you trying to ask me if I'm gay?'

'Well—are you?'

'On the principle that anyone who doesn't try to rush you into bed is pointing in the other direction? Hm! Well, it's a thought.'

'*Are you?*'

'Would it matter?'

'Of course it would matter. How could you advise me about him if you—?'

'Well, maybe he is too.'

'Is he?'

'How would I know? I've never propositioned him.'

She glared at him. 'Have I been wasting my time?'

'Doesn't your womanly intuition tell you one way or the other?' He was getting his own back now and it felt great. 'Am I not interested, or am I simply the perfect gentleman? Strange how hard it is to tell the difference these days.'

'You're enjoying this, aren't you?' she fumed.

'You bet I am. And why shouldn't I? The joke's been on me all this time, now it's your turn.'

'What do you mean? How has the joke been on you?'

With his feet at the very edge of the precipice, he pulled back sharply. He'd forgotten how little she knew.

'Nothing,' he said quickly.

'It must have meant something.'

'Then I'll just leave you to wonder. And in the meantime—Olympia—Olympia?'

The speed with which she'd switched her attention away from him would have been comic if it hadn't been dismaying. Now she was looking out into the semi-darkness on the dance floor.

'What is it?' he asked, taking her hand and squeezing it to get her attention.

'Nothing, I—I must have imagined it.'

'Whatever you imagined seems to have upset you. Can't you tell me?'

'I just thought I saw someone I knew—but in this light I'm probably mistaken.'

Unconsciously her hand had tightened on his until he winced from the pressure.

'Who is it?' he asked.

'My ex-husband.'

CHAPTER SIX

HE STARED at her. 'Your ex? Are you sure?'

'Yes, that's David—I think.'

'Does it matter?' he asked, shocked to realise that she was trembling. 'It's not as though you still love him—do you?'

'No, of course not. But it's the first time I've seen him since we split. Perhaps it isn't him,' she added, almost hopefully.

'But you can't be easy until you're sure?'

Suddenly her carefully honed confidence deserted her. 'What can I do? I can't walk over there and take a look.'

'You can if we're dancing.'

'But—'

'Olympia, you've got to do this. If you flunk it you'll never be able to look yourself in the mirror again.'

She knew it, but she was too nervous to think straight.

'Let's leave it,' she whispered. 'The past is the past.'

His hand tightened over hers. 'Nonsense. The past is never the past until you've faced it and told it to get the hell out of your way. What happened to the ''can do'' tycoon I've got to know?'

'She turned into a ''can't do'' wimp,' she said with a shaky laugh.

'No, she didn't. She just needs a friend to take her hand, like this.'

Giving her no chance to refuse, he drew her to her feet and on to the dance floor.

With a shock Olympia realised that he was finally holding her. So many times he could have taken her into his arms, and so many times he'd refused. Now he'd done so under the guise of a dance. But that was what dancing was for—to embrace, to hold each other closely and feel the pressure of each other's body and the exchange of warm breath, without admitting that was what you were doing.

'Which way?' he murmured, his breath brushing her cheek.

'Near the orchestra.'

Closer and closer they went while her eyes searched the tables at the edge of the dance floor until she found what she was seeking.

Her first thought was to wonder how she'd ever recognised him. David was plumper, sleeker, beginning to lose his hair, and there was an expression of discontent on his face that mirrored that of the woman sitting near him.

Rosalie! It took Olympia a moment to identify this stodgy creature with the elegant nymph who had persisted in her memory, but this was Rosalie now.

'Is that him?' her partner asked.

'I think—yes, it is.'

'And the woman with him?'

'Rosalie, his wife.'

'He made a bad bargain when he traded you for her,' said her friend.

Now Olympia saw that there were six people at the table. David's father-in-law was there with his wife, David and Rosalie, and two men who Olympia guessed were business contacts being entertained. One of them asked Rosalie to dance. Smiling, she took the floor with him.

It seemed to Olympia that there was an element of relief in that smile, as though anything was better than her husband's company.

As she glided around the floor in her partner's arms, David watched them sourly.

Suddenly the movements of the dance brought Olympia close to the couple. Rosalie's eyes flickered vacantly over Olympia before moving on to the man holding her in his arms. She seemed suddenly interested, turning her head as she moved, trying to keep him in view. Only at the last minute did she really seem to notice Olympia and then there was a shocked look in her eyes, disbelief, almost outrage.

'She didn't know you at first,' Primo whispered, 'but she does now.'

'I guess I've changed a bit since those days.'

The dance ended and the other couple headed back to their table. But the next dance started at once and Olympia found herself whirled into it without a by-your-leave.

His hand was in the small of her back, holding her close against him as his legs moved against hers. The sight of David had been a shock, bringing back sharp memories that she'd spent years banishing, but, faced with the reality, they were fast fading. It was hard to be aware of anything but the man swinging her around and around, holding her so close that their bodies were as one.

The room was whirling about her, making her cling to him as the only fixed point in the world. He'd said he was her friend, and that was partly why she held him so eagerly. And partly it wasn't that at all. Everything seemed to vanish but his face. She must make him stop this, but she wanted him never to stop.

At last he slowed and the room came back into focus. Now, she could see David again, listening to Rosalie, who was talking to him with animation and pointing back on to the floor. He rose and they started to dance together.

'She's told him,' Primo murmured. 'Now he wants to see for himself if it's you. Look, they're working their way towards us.'

'Oh, no!' she said involuntarily.

'Why "oh, no!"? This is your moment of triumph.'

'Is it?'

'Isn't it? Look at them. Sad and middle-aged before their time because they've made too many compromises, betrayed too many people. Then look at you, young and beautiful as a mermaid, every man's head turned to you in admiration. They've had it, and now it tastes sour. You've got it all before you, and it's going to be great.'

'Yes,' she breathed excitedly. 'Oh, yes!'

'Let him find out what he threw away. Make him sorry he let you go. Then hold your head high and walk out of here with me.'

'You're right.'

Again there was that *frisson* of excitement at how totally he understood her, as though their minds were linked even more closely than their bodies.

Closer and closer they danced until she was a couple of feet away from the man who had once filled her world, then broken her heart when he'd declared her not up to standard.

As Jack had promised, there was satisfaction in seeing the shock in his face as he recognised her. Her partner kept her there, dancing on the spot so that David could be in no doubt who he was seeing. Olympia met David's eyes in a moment of blazing victory.

'Look up at me,' said a voice close to her ear.

She did so, and immediately felt his lips on hers. She gasped, almost stumbling, but his arms held her safe, keeping her in the dance so that her feet seemed to move of their own accord while her mouth relished his.

It meant nothing, she thought desperately. He was a friend, helping her to make a point to David, boosting her pride like the true friend he was. She must accept his kiss in the same spirit, keeping a cool head, ignoring the wild feelings that went through her.

'Is he watching?' she gasped against his mouth.

'His eyes are on stalks,' he murmured back. 'And so are hers. Let's give them a repeat run. Kiss me—as though you really meant it.'

'*Right!*'

Her arms slid up about his neck, one hand curving pleasurably against his head, drawing him down to her, ready for him, eager for him. She did as he'd said, giving it everything as though she meant it, and felt his answering response.

Now he'd released her hand and tightened both arms around her, holding her so that she would have been helpless to resist, if that was what she'd wanted. But she had no thought of resistance. Her body had been aching for this, longing to know how it would feel to be held by him, and all the time she had been denying her instincts the need had been building within her.

If only they were not in public so that she could yield to the need that was overwhelming her, the need to touch him again and again and offer herself to his touch.

But that was what she mustn't do, she thought wildly. Being alone with him would tempt her to reveal too much. Touch would follow touch, deeper and more intimate until touching wasn't enough.

However hard it was, she must try to keep her distance. But this felt like a very strange way of keeping her distance.

He released her just enough for her head to fall back so that she was looking into his face. He seemed to be frowning as though some-thing had startled him, and she understood that reaction because she felt the same.

'What's happening?' she whispered.

'I'm not—quite—sure—'

And suddenly the world seemed to burst in a glitter of flashlights. People cheered, champagne bottles popped, red roses fell on them. Olympia saw that they were surrounded by waiters, all waving champagne and cheering.

'What on earth—?' she said.

A man in a glittering coat, who seemed to be the Master of Ceremonies, made his way towards them and bowed.

'Congratulations!' he cried. 'You are tonight's winners.'

'Winners at what?' she asked hazily.

'In our Lovers Competition. Every night this week, one lucky couple is declared our Premier Lovers—'

'But we're not lo—' she started to say, then gave up. She was being drowned out by cheering.

'Jack, what are we going to do?'

'Put up with it,' he said, close to her ear. 'We've no choice. It'll be over in a minute and we can slip away. In the meantime, try to look convincing. Smile. This is where the movie queen gives the hero the full power of her dazzling orbs and he goes weak at the knees.'

'Don't do that,' she begged. 'You're holding me up.'

He gave a crack of laughter, his eyes gleaming in appreciation of the joke.

The Master of Ceremonies was shouting, 'That was the most impressive kiss anyone's ever seen. How about another?'

Another cheer went up and the crowd began to chant, 'Kiss—kiss—'

'Jack—'

'We'll have to give them what they want, or they won't let us go,' he murmured.

'But we—'

'It can't be helped. Lie back and think of England.'

'You cheeky—'

'Hush,' he said, lowering his mouth to hers.

He was right. Who needed words when there were feelings like this? She gave herself up to what was happening, while all around them the crowd cheered and clapped.

When at last he released her she had a vision of David's face. It was a vacuous face, she realised, especially now, with his jaw dropping.

She had beaten him. The man who'd rejected her as dowdy and dull, who'd betrayed her love for money, had been made to regret it.

And she couldn't have cared less.

The Master of Ceremonies was dancing around them.

'It's wonderful what people will do to make sure they win,' he carolled.

'We didn't—' Olympia said breathlessly. 'We didn't know there was a contest.'

'You mean you normally act like that? Hey, folks, did you hear that? Boy, are these some lovers!'

More cheers, more applause.

'Can we sit down?' the Master of Ceremonies asked. 'Then we can sort out the details.'

She wanted to ask, what details? But she couldn't think clearly. Her legs were trembling, as though all the strength had drained away.

When they were seated at the table the Master of Ceremonies poured champagne and toasted them.

'And now for the big moment,' he said, 'when you get to choose your prize from among our glorious range. There's this—' He produced a catalogue showing some very fancy and high-priced entertainment equipment.

'Or there's this, a fortnight for two at a luxury health spa. Or two gift vouchers for the most expensive store in London. Or a vacation in any town in Europe, flights, hotel, the lot.'

He finished with an expansive gesture, like a man expecting applause. Primo indicated Olympia.

'It's her choice,' he said. 'Why don't you take the gift vouchers and blow the lot on clothes?'

'Oh, no,' she said. 'I've got a much better idea. I'll take the trip to Europe.'

'Wonderful!' the Master of Ceremonies exclaimed. 'And which city shall it be?'

Olympia smiled at Primo.

'Naples,' she said.

On the drive home he said, 'What do you want to happen about David? Shall I get Leonate to buy out his firm and fire him? Or employ him? Say the word.'

'No need,' she said contentedly. 'If I wanted revenge, I've had it. I'm so glad that happened. He really is in the past now. Thank you. You knew just what to do.'

'Good. Then can we talk about Naples?'

She gave a soft laugh. 'Your face was a picture!'

'I'll bet it was. You were winding me up, weren't you? Good joke.'

'That man said the Vallini Hotel was the best. Do you know it?'

'Yes, it's about halfway up the hill, overlooking the bay. It costs a fortune just to walk past it.'

'I like the sound of that,' she said with a sigh.

'But you weren't serious, were you?' he asked, sounding slightly alarmed.

Choosing not to answer this, she diplomatically closed her eyes and pretended to doze for the rest of the journey.

When they reached home he came upstairs with her, and it was only when they were in her apartment that she said, 'Actually, I wasn't joking back there. I'm going to Naples and I'm going to stay in that luxury hotel while I look around. I'm due for some time off. I haven't had any for ages, and you can authorise it. It's simple.'

'It's not a good idea.'

'It's a wonderful idea. It's fate. And after what happened tonight I'm even more certain that this happened because it had to.'

After what happened tonight. That stopped him in his tracks.

'Jack, I've been doing a lot of thinking— about the way things are going.'

'I know,' he said slowly.

'You know what I want and how determined I am to get it. It doesn't make me a nice person, but I can't change. I simply have to go for my goal.'

'Primo Rinucci. But he isn't here.'

'I know. And he's never going to be here, I see that now. So I must go to him.'

'*What?*'

'That's what I mean about fate. I can work on my Italian, learn some Neapolitan. It'll give me better chances than staying here.'

'But what about Curtis? It was your ambition to take over.'

'Well, maybe the world doesn't begin and end with Curtis. Maybe I'm broadening my horizons.'

'Which means—?' he asked suspiciously.

'Ambition alone is not enough,' she declared with the air of someone quoting eternal truth. 'Ambition plus flexibility yields results.'

He stared at her. 'Who said that?'

'I did.'

'I mean, who said it first?'

'I did. You just heard me.'

He passed a hand over his eyes, trying to get control of his thoughts.

'You sounded as though you were quoting an authority,' he explained.

'I was. Me.'

'Oh, well, in that case—!' he said wildly. 'Why not jot it down and put it in a book when you're running the Stock Exchange? *Notes On How I Did It.* You too can rule the world. Just roll over everyone like a steamroller.'

'How dare you call me a steam-roller!'

'It's that or a three ton tractor. Take your pick.'

'Jack, where's your spirit of adventure?'

'It passed out under the table in the night-club, and as far as I'm concerned it can stay there. Olympia, what's got into you? It's bad enough for you to be laying traps for this poor fool—'

'Don't call my benefactor a fool!'

'So now he's your benefactor?'

'He will be, when I've finished with him.'

'Then he *is* a fool,' he said recklessly. 'And so are you for hunting him down, because it'll frighten him off.'

'He won't even know. I'll just turn up in Naples, look around—'

'You're out of your mind.'

'You mean you won't help me?'

He took her shoulders, shaking her very slightly as though this would get him into her head.

'Olympia, you're living in a dream world. It's a delightful fantasy, but not if it means turning your back on what's happening be-tween us.'

'We're having a pleasant flirtation. It's lovely, but it doesn't lead anywhere. We enjoy each other's company and then pass on. That's always been the deal.'

'I don't remember making any deal.'

'I was always honest with you. You knew my terms and you didn't refuse them.'

'Then I guess I just hoped you'd soon see things a bit more clearly. I don't think it's all on my side. Look me in the eye and tell me you don't feel anything for me.'

'After tonight, I can't. But I won't *let* it happen. I felt something like that once before, and I know where it leads.'

'I know where it would have led if you'd stayed with him. You saw him in the night-club. You saw his wife, what marriage to him has turned her into. Be glad you escaped.'

'I am glad, but that's hindsight. All that kind of thing is over for me. You've always known that.'

'All right, I've known it, but I've tried not to believe it. And I won't believe it now. You keep trying to make me think badly of you—'

'I want you to see me as I am,' she flashed. 'I'm hard and cold—'

'You weren't hard and cold in my arms tonight.'

'That'll never happen again. I won't let it.'

'Stop it,' he said fiercely, seizing her in his arms and giving her a little shake. 'Don't talk like that. I forbid you.'

'Who are you to forbid me?'

His answer was to tighten his grip and pull her hard against him, kissing her with something close to ferocity.

For a moment she tensed against him, but then her refusal melted in the warmth and sweetness he could inspire in her with such treacherous ease.

'This is who I am,' he murmured against her lips. 'Don't you recognise me now?'

'Yes,' she whispered, kissing him back.

'You know me—you know me—'

She knew him. He was the one who haunted her dreams, resisting all attempts to banish him. She would escape him now while she still could—while there was time—but there was no time—

She kissed him again and again, each time promising that this would be the last.

'How can you leave when we have this?' he demanded hoarsely.

'Don't you see, it's because we *could* have this that I'm doing what must be done.'

'You mean you're running,' he said scornfully. 'Running like a coward who's afraid of life.'

The words were bitter, brutal, but he couldn't help it. The pain of her rejection was intense.

'Maybe I am,' she said. 'But I don't want to feel all that again, Jack, and you frighten me. You could take me to a place where I don't want to be—'

'If we were there together, like tonight—'

'It will never happen again. *I won't let it.*'

He drew apart from her, gasping.

'Wait here,' he said through gritted teeth, and walked out of the room without a backward glance.

He went all the way downstairs before he called Italy on his cellphone, taking no chance of being overheard. First he called Cedric Tandy.

'Cedric, I know it's late but I need a favour from you—'

It was a short call, very satisfactory, and ended with him saying, 'Cedric, you're a lifesaver. Go back to bed now.'

Next he spoke to Enrico, who wasn't best pleased at being hauled out of bed, but who also agreed to what Primo wanted, because people always did. After nearly half an hour he returned to Olympia. Secretly he was glad she'd forced the issue, driving him to a decision.

'It's settled,' he said when he rejoined her. 'I've been telling them about you and Leonate wants me to take you out there so that he can get to know you.'

'And what then?'

'You'll work in Naples for a while, then in a few months you'll know what you want to do. You may decide you want to return here and run Curtis. If so, you'll make a better job of it for having worked at the centre of things. Or you may decide that you like Naples and want to keep your job there.'

'What about you?'

'I'm flying out with you and staying for a while, to see you settled in, but I won't be living at the hotel. I have an apartment.'

'Wait, I can't get my head round this. Who'll run Curtis while you're away?'

'Cedric. His retirement package contains an option for another six months.'

'Does it? I saw it and I didn't see anything about another six months.'

'It's a recent development,' he said hurriedly, not choosing to tell her how recent. 'It gives me a breather while I make decisions about his replacement. He won't mind if I invoke that option. It keeps your options open too.

'And now that we've settled everything, I'll leave.' His voice became brisk. 'I want you in the office first thing tomorrow. There are arrangements to be made. Is your passport in order?'

'Of course.'

'Have you got the number that man in the disgusting jacket gave you to ring when you'd settled the date?'

'Of course.'

'Fine. Tell them we'll travel in two days. We'll sort out the final details tomorrow. Goodnight.'

He left without another word.

Olympia stood watching the closed door, feeling more confused than she'd been in her life. He threatened her peace, and she'd told herself that the time had come to escape him. But somehow he'd wrested control from her. The trip to Naples would be on his terms.

She'd outwitted him—and then she hadn't.

Suddenly the future was more exciting than it had ever been.

As he'd said it was all systems go in the office next morning.

'How can you leave so soon, when you've barely got here?' Olympia protested.

'But I'm only obeying orders,' he said innocently. 'Just a humble cog in the Leonate wheel, doing as I'm told, that's me.'

'Why don't I find that convincing?'

'Maybe you're just not a very good judge of character,' he said simply.

From then on packing and making arrangements about her apartment occupied all her time, and when she finally closed the door to start the journey to the airport she hadn't seen him for two days. She had to take a taxi. He didn't even bother to collect her.

She was glad of the time apart. It gave her a breathing space to get her ideas together and remind herself what really mattered. He was attractive, no doubt about it, but so what? She could enjoy a flirtation without compromising her mission, couldn't she?

But then these cool thoughts would be invaded by memories that were anything but cool: the way he'd held her in his arms, the fierce crushing kiss with a hint of some suppressed feeling that might have been desperation, the skilled movements of his lips, knowing so well how to incite her to respond.

He knew her too well. He could speak to her in a silent language they both understood. He was dangerous. She must escape him.

But she was glad with all her heart that he was coming with her.

He was waiting at the airport, greeting her with an air of tension that puzzled her.

'Are you all right?' she asked.

'Fine, fine. Just not too keen on flying.'

In fact he was an excellent traveller, but he'd just completed what he promised himself would be the last, the very last piece of trickery.

Realising that his ticket would be provided in the name of Cayman, he'd intercepted it when it had been delivered to the office the previous day, then booked himself another ticket in his true name and got to the airport early to collect it.

Now he was vowing that it would all soon be over. Safe in Naples, he would confess everything to Olympia over a glass of wine. They would share a laugh, and she would forgive him.

Eventually.

And he would never tell another lie as long as he lived. His nerves couldn't stand it.

CHAPTER SEVEN

'THERE it is,' he said as the volcano came into view in the distance. 'That's what you've been watching for, isn't it?'

'Vesuvius,' she said ecstatically. 'How fierce and magnificent it looks.'

The plane turned and now the lights of Naples were below them, like arms curving around the bay. Another few minutes and they were down.

Then they were in the taxi, climbing the hill to the Vallini, the grandest hotel that Naples had to offer. As soon as she stepped through the door she was enveloped in luxury. Uniformed staff murmured, *'Signorina,'* as they ushered her to her suite.

There she found a double bed of antique design but modern comfort, a marble bathroom and a sitting room with a balcony that looked out over the bay.

'I'll leave you for a while,' he said, 'while I check my apartment. I'll be back in a couple of hours.'

When he'd gone she had a long soak in scented water while the hotel laundry service pressed the creases from the black dress she'd worn to the nightclub. A hairdresser arrived and dressed her long black hair in elegant sweeps, some wound about her head, some falling.

It was a magical evening. He led her downstairs to his low slung sports car.

'Let me show you a little of my town,' he said.

They drove for an hour through narrow cobbled streets. Once she caught him stealing a smiling glance at her and knew it was a reminder of how he'd once teased her about 'urchins and cobbled streets'.

'But where are the urchins?' she asked at last and they both laughed.

They dined at a tiny *trattoria,* saying little. He forbade her to speak English and she struggled through the evening with her basic Italian.

'You're doing well,' he said. 'The more you practise it the better.'

'When do I start work?' she wanted to know.

'Let's enjoy a few days holiday first. Once I've introduced you to Enrico you'll be swallowed up.' After a moment he added delicately, 'And, of course, there's the other introduction you want.'

'Oh, yes,' she murmured. 'Him.'

For a moment she'd wondered who he meant.

'Yes, him,' he said, eyebrows slightly raised. 'Primo Rinucci. The man this is all about.'

'Well, there's no rush, is there? Let's not talk about him tonight. I don't want to think about work.'

'I'll swear it's years since you last said that.'

'Yes,' she said in surprise. 'It is.'

She wondered how anyone could think of work in this colourful place. Looking through the window by their table, she saw couples strolling through the narrow streets, lost in each other. It had been raining earlier and the blurred reflections of lights gleamed on the wet cobbles, giving a misty edge to the world. No, tonight she didn't want to think of work, or anything except the man with her.

She listened for the voice telling her to beware because he endangered her ambitions, but somehow it was muted. She would listen to it another time.

'What are you thinking?' he asked.

'You wouldn't believe me if I told you.'

'Then don't tell me. I'll work it out.'

'I wonder if you will.'

'I will, *strega*. I will.'

'*Strega?*'

'There are still gaps in your Italian. Look it up.'

'Tell me.'

'No.' He shook his head, his lips pressed firmly together. 'But I've thought of you as *strega* since the first day.'

'Is it a nice thing to be?'

'It changes. Mostly it leaves me not knowing what to think.'

'And that annoys you?'

'Only sometimes. At others—' He let the implication hang in the air.

'Tell me,' she begged again, but he only shook his head.

He drove slowly back to the hotel and saw her up to her suite.

'Go to bed and sleep well,' he said. 'I'll call early tomorrow.'

'Come for breakfast.'

'All right. And we'll plan the day. There's a lot I want to show you. Look—'

He led the way out on to the balcony where a brilliant full moon shone down over the bay. She stared out over the dark water, unable to believe such beauty.

His cellphone rang and he muttered something rude, turning back into the room to answer it. The next moment she heard his shocked exclamation.

Hurrying back into the room, she saw him standing with the phone to his ear, his eyes wide, his jaw gaping.

'What is it?' she asked urgently.

'OK, Cedric,' he said into the phone. 'Look, don't worry about it. It's not your fault. I'll take care of it. Don't blame yourself. I'm coming. Just hang in there.'

'You're going back to England?' she asked.

'Only for a couple of days. Do you remember a man called Norris Banyon?'

'Yes, he ran the accounts department, but he left suddenly a couple of weeks ago. I never liked him.'

'With reason, it seems. He was fiddling the books for years.'

'But how could he get away with it? Leonate had a firm of accountants swarming all over the books before you made your offer. They said everything was all right.'

'Yes, but Banyon had had time to cover his tracks, and he was there, day by day, thinking on his feet, always ready with an explanation for any question they raised. But as soon as the deal was concluded he left, taking a large sum with him. And, of course, the minute he was gone it began to unravel.

'Is it disastrous?'

'No, it won't bring us down or anything. But Cedric blames himself.'

'That's not fair.'

'No, it isn't. I have to go back to calm him down. I'll get some more accountants in—a different firm this time—and they'll sort it out. Then I'll cheer poor old Cedric up. Since his wife died last year he's been alone. He has no children or close family, so there's nobody at home to help him cope.'

Olympia stared. She hadn't known Cedric's wife had died.

'That's really nice of you,' she said.

'Well, Cedric—er—did me a big favour recently.' He cleared his throat awkwardly.

'I'll come too.'

'Better not,' he said quickly.

'But I was his assistant. I can help with this.'

'He'd hate for you to know. I'll be back in a few days, when I've hired the new auditors. Until then, enjoy being a tourist and get to know my city.' He looked at his watch. 'There's a plane at dawn. I'd better go now.'

'You mean this minute?' she asked, horrified.

'I don't want to go but I think I must.'

'Of course. Give him my love.'

But she could have wept with disappointment. Something had started to happen, something that wasn't supposed to happen, and which she'd foolishly resisted. Now she was no longer resisting and she could see the road stretching out ahead, uncertain but inviting. Just not yet.

He hesitated over saying goodbye, holding her hand in his. At last he laid a gentle kiss on her mouth and hurried away. From the balcony she could see him leave the hotel, get into his car and drive away down the hill.

She looked back at her suite, the epitome of luxury, a symbol of the place she had wanted to be. But there was nobody there with her.

She thought of Cedric, too uptight to talk about his loneliness with the people he'd known for years. But Jack had known and responded with kindness.

He called her on the evening of the next day, telling her that things weren't as bad as they'd sounded, and he'd persuaded Cedric to stop beating his breast.

'I'll be with you soon,' he said. 'How are you occupying your time without me?'

'Reading dictionaries,' she said.

His voice reached her down the line, warm and amused, thrilling her from a distance of a thousand miles. 'So now you know what *strega* means. Do you like it?'

'Yes, I think I do. It could be interesting. But I won't know until you come back.'

'It'll be as soon as I can manage. And when I'm there we have a lot to talk about.'

'I know. Come back soon.'

When she'd hung up she sat looking at the phone, seeming to hear his voice in the air about her. For a moment the sensation was so strong that she nearly reached out, sure that she could touch him.

There was a suspicious wetness in her eyes and on her cheeks. She brushed it away, then went to bed and lay awake dreaming about him.

She whiled away the time by exploring Naples, but after the first day she was so footsore that she hired a car.

She went out into the countryside, stopped to eat at small inns and drove back as late as possible, trying to convince herself that she was having a good time. The land was beautiful, the bay was astonishing, but it was all wrong because *he* wasn't here.

She'd told herself that she must run from him, but running was useless. He could give her the kind of feelings she'd sworn never to know again, and to rejoice in them. That knowledge would be waiting around every corner.

And he knew. Of course he did. He'd played along with the joke, waiting for her to get over her fantasies and reach out to the real man. It had happened, and all could be well, except that it had happened in the wrong way, at the wrong time, when he wasn't even here.

Perhaps she'd needed him to go, so that the ache of missing him told her what she wanted to know. But why, oh why, didn't he come back to her now?

Meanwhile she tried to occupy herself with being a tourist, but wherever she went she was thinking of him, planning how to tell him that she'd changed. How they would laugh together at the way she'd been overcome by her feelings! And then—

Every day she lunched at the *trattoria* where they'd eaten during his few brief hours here, at the same table if possible. Then she would search for something to fill the afternoon.

Despite all the historical sights, what attracted her most was the great building that was Leonate Europa. She longed to visit it, and even went so far as to turn into its underground car park. There she switched off the engine and sat behind the wheel, torn by temptation.

Surely it would do no harm to go in and introduce herself? After all, she'd signed a contract to work here. She could meet Enrico Leonate. She might even meet Primo Rinucci.

Then she smiled as she realised that she didn't care whether she met him or not. Only Jack counted now. Soon he would call to say he was returning. She would go to meet him at the airport and their time would come.

She started up the engine and began to edge her way out of the car park into the stream of traffic. It was late afternoon, the worst time of day to be driving. The traffic was at its most crowded and she was fast becoming confused by the car and everything around her. She remembered Jack attributing his accident to the fact that the English drove on the 'wrong' side of the road. Now she knew how he felt.

There was a blast on the horn from the driver behind her. Startled, she turned the car swiftly to the side, realising too late that she'd chosen the wrong one.

'Damn!' she muttered, trying to brake, turn and see where she was going, all at once. '*Oh, no!*'

A shadow had appeared on her windscreen, a shadow that vanished with alarming suddenness.

'Oh, no!' she cried again, flinging herself out of the car. 'What have I done?'

'Covered me with bruises,' said a man's voice from the ground. Mercifully he sounded robust, even amused.

'I didn't actually hit you, did I?'

'No, I jumped out of the way when you swerved, and missed my footing.' He climbed to his feet, moving gingerly. 'Those kerbs are very sharp when you fall on them,' he complained, rubbing his elbow.

A bellow of sound from behind reminded her that other drivers were waiting to move.

'I've got to go,' she said, 'but I can't just leave you here. Can you get into my car?'

'Why don't I drive it for you?'

'That might be better,' she said with relief. 'The roads in Naples are—I don't know—'

When they were in the car and he was guiding them through the traffic he said, 'It's not just Naples. The roads in the rest of Italy are pretty hair-raising too. You're not Italian, are you?'

'You guessed! Neither are you by the sound of it. English?'

'Let's say I started out that way. Nowadays I'm not sure what I am. What's your name?'

'Olympia Lincoln.'

'Luke Cayman.'

'Cayman?' She looked at him quickly. 'Are you any relation to Jack Cayman?'

Before he could answer, a sleek sports car swept right in front of them, forcing Luke to brake sharply and utter a stream of Neapolitan curses. By the time things had sorted themselves out with lots of honking and bawling, Luke had had time to catch his breath and partly understand the situation.

Now, if ever, was the moment to watch every word. Brother Stuffed-Shirt Primo had certainly been up to something. But what? That was the million dollar question that he was going to enjoy exploring.

'Sorry,' he said at last. 'What was the name?'

'Jack Cayman. I met him in England. He works for Leonate. Surely you must be related? Two Englishmen with the same name, in Naples.'

As his thoughts settled he realised that he might have overreacted. Primo sometimes used his father's name for wheeling and dealing in England, thinking it would make him less conspicuous. It might mean nothing.

'It sounds like my brother,' he mused.

'Your brother?'

'That's right. We both come from England originally.'

'Are you part of the firm too?'

'Leonate? Not part of, but I'm in the same line of electronics and I've just sold them some goods, so I'd just dropped in to sign the papers. Jack and I don't see much of each other because he travels a lot. Look, I know a little *trattoria* just down here and I need some sustenance after the fright you gave me.'

She suppressed a childish desire to say, Oh, yeah? The mere idea of this man taking fright was incongruous. He was like a rock. A pleasant, attractive rock, but a rock just the same. It was there in the shape of his head and his jaw line.

When at last they were seated, eating pizza and drinking coffee, he said, 'I never take my car when I visit Leonate. The roads near it are so bad that it's quicker on foot. But how did you come to be driving out of that building?'

'I work there—well, sort of. I come from Curtis in England.'

'So you've been taken over?'

'I suppose I have. I'm here to learn the business and the language, and anything else I can.'

'Was that Jack's idea?'

'Mine mainly. I sort of forced his hand.'

'You—forced Pr—forced *his* hand?' Luke asked carefully. 'Not an easy man to force.'

She nodded. 'I wanted to come to Naples. A way presented itself and in the end he saw things my way.'

To Olympia's amazement Luke threw his head back and roared with laughter.

'You don't know how it sounds to hear you say that,' he said at last. 'That's how he talks—do it my way. And people always do, because he gives them no choice. I guess you've heard him.'

'No, I've never heard him say that,' she said. 'It doesn't sound like him at all.'

'Doesn't *sound*—? We can't be talking about the same man. Is something the matter?'

He'd noticed her looking over his shoulder and turned, half expecting to find Primo.

Instead, it was his mother that he saw standing just inside the door, trying to attract his attention.

'Mamma!' He rose to embrace her and she hugged him back enthusiastically.

'I've been trying to call you, but you turned your phone off,' she reproved him. 'Now introduce me to your friend.'

'Mamma, this is Miss Olympia Lincoln. Miss Lincoln, this is my mother.'

Olympia regarded the newcomer with admiration. She looked between fifty and sixty, with an elegant figure and a face that was a tribute to the power of the massage parlour. She was fighting off encroaching age, and doing it very skilfully.

She shook hands with Olympia, giving her the welcoming but sharp-eyed look of a mother with too many unmarried sons. She evidently liked what she saw, for her smile broadened.

'Mamma, sit down and have coffee with us,' Luke said.

'I have no time. I must hurry back to the villa to finish preparations for tonight.' To

Olympia she said, 'We're having a family party and you must come.'

'Oh, no—thank you, but—if it's a family party—'

'Of course you must come. I won't take no for an answer. Luke, you hear me now and bring this nice girl to us tonight.'

She paused to regard Olympia with admiration.

'We'll have some dancing and I just know you'll look wonderful in a long dress.'

'Mamma!' Luke covered his eyes.

'Well, she will. Crimson, I think.'

'Crimson?' Olympia exclaimed in surprise. 'I've never thought of it as my colour.'

'But it is. You must wear crimson, if not tonight then the next time I see you.'

She kissed Luke and hurried out before either of them could answer.

'You do realise that you've just been given your orders, don't you?' Luke said with a grin. 'Mamma's rather overwhelming, but she means it kindly.'

'I know she does, and she's made me feel so welcome.'

Luke suppressed the thought that this was because Hope was preparing to swallow Olympia alive in the name of 'acquiring daughters-in-law', and merely said, 'You will come, won't you? Just to keep her happy? She always gets cross if her sons turn up without girlfriends. She accuses us of only associating with the kind of girls a man can't take home to his mother.'

'Rightly?' Olympia asked, her eyes full of fun.

He cleared his throat. 'It's a long story. She thinks she's right and I just go along with it. We all do. But boy, does she ask a lot of questions! I swear it's like being interrogated by the Inquisition, but if you're there I'll be spared.'

'You won't, you know,' she chuckled. 'You'll just be asked a different kind of question, and probably twice as many.'

He groaned. 'How horribly true!'

'Questions are what mothers do,' she said sympathetically. 'One way or the other.'

'But you will come, won't you? It's the least you can do after knocking me down.'

'All right,' she said, laughing.

It would be better than spending the evening alone, wondering when Jack would return. She had tried to call him earlier but his cellphone had been switched off.

Luke drove her back to the Vallini and whistled at the sight of her destination. Once inside she went straight to the hire shop, seeking a suitable dress for that night. She was resolute in her determination to make her own choice, but somehow the gown that suited her best just happened to be deep crimson satin. She hired it and some gold jewellery, then bought gold sandals to go with it.

When the hairdresser had come to her suite and whipped up her hair into an elaborate confection, she was ready for the evening.

She tried to call Jack, but for the third time she couldn't get through. She frowned, puzzled by the odd silence and wishing with all her heart that he could be here and see her looking like this.

His brother was nice, but it was chiefly his relationship to Jack that made him so. She would see the house which had been their home and learn something about him.

If only he could be here, she thought sadly, regarding the vision in the mirror that he wouldn't see.

Luke's frank admiration was balm to her soul, although he couldn't resist saying, 'You'll give Mamma ideas, dressing like that.'

'It's not because of anything she said. This was the perfect dress. She was right about that.'

'I'll believe you. She won't.'

'Is it far?' she asked, diplomatically changing the subject.

'No distance. Just at the top of this hill. You'll see it as soon as we're on the road.'

Just as he'd said, the family home loomed up above them as they climbed the hill. All the lights were on and they seemed to blaze out a welcome over the whole of the surrounding city, the countryside, the bay, even as far as Vesuvius.

'When you're up there the volcano looks very near because there's nothing in between but clear air,' Luke told her. 'The least little murmur from Vesuvius, the tiniest puff of smoke, seems to be happening right on top of you.'

'You mean things happen even these days?'

'Nothing to worry about. The old man gives the odd grumble from deep in the earth, just to remind us not to take him for granted, but the last actual eruption was sixty years ago. Toni's father saw it happen and he used to warn us always to tell the truth, because Vesuvius was listening and would growl with displeasure if we offended. So every time there was the faintest murmur we all used to jump nervously.'

At last they swung into the great courtyard of the villa. As they left the car a door in the house opened and his mother emerged, throwing up her arms in joyful greeting.

'Mamma!' Luke called cheerfully, climbing the steps, Olympia's hand in his. 'You see, I've brought her.'

His mother gave him a perfunctory kiss before welcoming Olympia eagerly, her eyes flickering over the red dress.

'Perfect,' she said. 'It suits you, as I knew it would.'

'It's just an accident that she chose that dress, Mamma,' Luke said quickly. 'She told me so.'

'Of course she did. Olympia, my dear, you are very welcome. Now come and meet the rest of my family.'

As Olympia went into the house Hope drew Luke aside, murmuring, 'She'll make a beautiful bride.'

'Mamma, you don't know her.'

'I can tell these things. She *looks* like my daughter-in-law.'

'For which one of us?' he asked, amused.

'Whichever one she will deign to have,' Hope informed him caustically. 'She may take her pick.'

'Oh, no,' he said at once. 'She's all mine.'

'Congratulations, my son. Your taste is improving.'

As they entered the warm house Olympia turned towards her. 'Mrs Cayman—'

Luke's mother laughed. 'Oh, my dear, I'm sorry. We're all so casual about names. I'm not Mrs Cayman any more. That was years ago. I'm Signora Rinucci.'

'Rinucci? You mean—?'

'Toni's name is Rinucci, and this is the Villa Rinucci.'

'Then—you know Primo Rinucci?'

'My stepson. He should have been here to-night but he was called back to England very suddenly. But of course, if you work for Leonate you must know him.'

'No, I don't. Somehow we've always just missed each other.'

'Wait a moment,' said Hope, going to a cup-board and reaching inside.

She brought out a large photo album and laid it down on a small table, turning the heavy pages until she came to a picture and pointed to it.

'That's him,' she said triumphantly.

Smiling, Olympia gazed down at the face of Primo Rinucci. And her smile faded.

CHAPTER EIGHT

FOR a long moment Olympia felt absolutely nothing. What she was seeing was so impossible that there could be no reaction.

Her hostess was explaining, 'Primo was the son of my first husband, Jack Cayman. His mother was a Rinucci and he took the family name when he came to live here.'

Olympia barely heard the words. Her stomach was churning as the dreadful truth finally became real, sharp. This was Primo Rinucci. The man she had trusted, confided in, to whom she had revealed her whole ambitious strategy, had been keeping this secret all the time.

What a laugh she must have given him!

'So that's Primo,' she said at last, surprised to find that she could speak normally. 'No, I don't know him.'

She fought to remain calm. Nobody must suspect that she'd received a shattering blow. That would be to pile disaster on disaster.

Instead she would smile and smile, concealing the turmoil in her heart.

'I never knew him,' she repeated quietly.

It was true. She'd thought she knew him so well, but all the time he'd been a stranger. The affectionate friend she'd trusted had never existed, because he'd been laughing at her, encouraging her to confide in him as she'd never done with anyone before, making a fool of her. When she thought of some of the things she'd said to him she went hot and cold.

Worst of all, she'd actually begun to believe that she might fall in love with him. And all the time he'd been sitting back, enjoying the situation at her expense.

She must hurry away from here, get back to England, leave the firm and go where she need never meet him again.

'There you two are,' Luke said, appearing beside his mother. 'Mamma, everyone's looking for you. There's some sort of crisis in the kitchen.'

When she had hurried away he glanced at Olympia, concerned. 'Are you all right?'

'I'm fine, fine!' she said brightly.

'Come and have some champagne and I'll introduce you to everyone.'

She followed like an automaton, while behind the façade her mind seethed.

She had only herself to blame because she'd always known he was a deceiver. That first day he'd pretended to be her secretary. Just a little tease, easy to pass off as a joke. But he hadn't told her until someone else had exposed him. It had been a warning she should have heeded.

Instead, she'd blundered on blindly, convincing herself that it was only a game. But the bitter hurt that consumed her now was shocking, terrifying, and she almost staggered under its impact.

After the first concerned question Luke hadn't spoken again. But he'd glimpsed the photograph and seen her horror. Now things were coming together in his mind and he had a suspicion of the truth.

So brother Primo had kicked over the traces, he mused. And with a vengeance!

He took her to meet his family—Toni, his father, his brothers, Toni's elderly parents who were paying them a visit and were guests of honour. There were also some business acquaintances.

Now Olympia seemed pervaded by a glacial calm that Luke found disturbing. He'd lived long enough in Italy to be comfortable with shouting and smashed plates. But freezing control made him uneasy.

'Do you want to talk about it?' he asked gently.

'There's nothing to talk about.'

'Well, my family are crazy about you, especially Mamma.'

'I think she's wonderful. She's been so nice to me.'

Someone called Luke's name and he turned briefly away. Olympia's eyes sought out Hope and found her at the exact moment Primo walked through the door.

She drew a sharp breath and turned away, hoping she'd hidden her face in time. He wasn't supposed to be here. Why hadn't he let her know he was coming back?

Had he noticed her? Please, no! She needed a moment to get control of herself so that she could meet him calmly. At all costs she must be the one in charge of this situation. Just a few more minutes and she would be strong enough to outface him.

Hope was eagerly hugging Primo, exclaiming over his early return.

'You made it! I thought you were going to be trapped in England for ages.'

'No, I got through everything at the speed of light,' he said. 'I just wanted to hurry back here.'

This was true. The thought of what might be happening in his absence was making him nervous.

'You're here in time for the excitement,' she told him. 'Luke brought a really nice girl tonight. She'll make him an excellent wife.'

'You know that already, do you?' he asked, grinning.

'I knew the moment I set eyes on her.'

'So all you have to do is persuade her.'

'I'm halfway there already. I suggested—in the mildest possible way, of course—that she would look wonderful in a long crimson dress. And tonight she turned up wearing the very thing. She wants the same thing that I want and that's her way of telling me.'

'And what about what Luke wants?' Primo asked with a grin. 'Has anyone thought of asking him, or will he just take what's supplied as long as it's stamped Approved by Mamma?'

'Don't be cheeky. He knows she's right for him. If you could have heard the way he spoke of her tonight, the way he said, ''She's all mine.'' Oh, it'll be wonderful to see him married. And then I must set to work on you.'

'Mamma, you set to work on me twenty years ago,' he said with a laugh.

'I want you to find a woman as perfect for you as this one is for Luke.'

'Well, that may have already happened.'

She gave a little shriek of joy. 'Is this the mystery woman, the one you've been dropping hints about and won't bring to meet your family?'

'How could I? We've been in England. But I'll bring her to meet you soon, I promise.'

'You've made up your mind?'

'Yes, definitely.'

She shrieked again and threw her arms around him.

'What's all the fuss?' Toni asked, appearing and clapping Primo on the shoulder.

'Primo's going to be married, and so's Luke,' Hope said ecstatically.

'I thought Luke only met her today,' Toni said. 'Isn't it a bit soon—?'

'What does time matter when two people are made for each other?' his wife reproved him. 'Perhaps we'll end up having a double wedding—Primo and his mystery woman, and Luke and his fiancée.'

'Mamma, will you calm down?' Primo begged. 'I can't even think of a wedding yet. There are—practical difficulties.'

'Well, if you're not careful, your brother will steal a march on you. Come and meet her.'

He followed her, happy to be home in the place he loved and wishing he could have brought Olympia with him. He had thought of her all the time he'd been away and every moment on the plane back. He'd even worked out how he would arrive without warning, take her by surprise and then tell her the truth.

But he'd reached her hotel to find that she'd gone out for the evening, nobody knew where. Resigned, he'd come to the party to please his mother, yet now he found his thoughts fixed on Olympia again. How he longed to bring her here openly to meet his family. He was smiling as he let his mother lead him across the room.

There was Luke in animated conversation with a young woman who stood with her back to Primo, her black hair elegantly dressed and streaming down her back in glossy waves.

That sight caused a nervous flinching inside him. Even from this angle there was something dreadfully familiar about her, but it couldn't be—it surely couldn't be—

Then she turned and the nightmare became real.

He was still some feet away from her and now that little distance seemed like a mile, going on for ever. He approached slowly, like a sleepwalker, transfixed, watching the ironic smile on her face until at last, after a long, long time, he stood before her.

'Olympia,' he murmured.

'*Signore!*' she murmured in return.

She was cool and composed, but her eyes warned him of trouble to come.

Hope embraced her.

'My dear, I want to introduce you to Primo, whom I was just telling you about. I can't believe you two haven't run across each other before.'

'Oh, no,' Olympia said silkily. 'I've never met Signor Rinucci before.'

She extended her hand and when he took it her fingers tightened in a grip that was painful, warning him to say nothing about the real situation. She needn't have worried. Nothing on earth would have persuaded him to tell anyone about this disaster.

'Never mind,' Hope exclaimed. 'The two of you have met now, and that's all that matters. *Yes, Toni, I'm coming!* I must see to my guests, but I'll be back.'

She hurried away, leaving the other two gazing steadily at each other.

'So you're Primo Rinucci,' Olympia mused, still smiling. 'I kept thinking I'd probably meet him before this, but somehow it never quite worked out. I'm not sure why.'

She gazed charmingly into his face, as though inviting him to speculate.

'Some things—are hard to explain,' he said vaguely.

'Oh, I don't think it's as hard as all that,' she said. 'Several reasons come to mind. I'm even a little surprised to meet him now, but it has all the charm of the unexpected, don't you think? Or perhaps charm is the wrong word.'

'Indeed,' he said vaguely.

He was trying to pull himself together, alarmed to notice that she seemed perfectly in command of the situation while he was floundering.

'Is that the best you can manage?' she asked. 'You don't have a lot to say for yourself, do you? Strange, I remember you as such a clever talker.'

'Olympia,' he whispered, 'please don't jump to conclusions.'

'I didn't jump to this conclusion. It bounded out and socked me on the jaw. Inside I'm still reeling, but some things become clear even when you're in a state of shock. Don't you find that?' Her tone expressed merely interest.

'I'm in a state of shock right now,' he said wryly. 'But your powers of recovery seem remarkable.'

'Yes, but I knew first. Your mother showed me your photograph and gave me your name.'

And then he realised her sharp wits had told her all she needed to know. Now she had him at a hopeless disadvantage.

He pulled himself together and tried to match her amused tone, saying, 'Personally I enjoy dealing with the unexpected. You can get some pleasant surprises that way.'

'And some nasty shocks,' she said coolly. 'Not to mention severe disappointments.'

'Isn't it a bit soon to judge that?'

'I don't think so. Some judgements are best made immediately.'

'And some can be made too soon,' he murmured.

In the soft light it was hard to be sure but he thought she went a little pale.

'Yes, I discovered that years ago,' she said. 'I thought I was past having to learn it again, but I was wrong.'

The throb of hurt in her voice made him draw a sharp breath.

'Don't confuse me with David,' he whispered. 'I'm not like him.'

'You're right. David was a cheapskate but he was honest in his way. At least I knew his name.'

'I never meant to hurt you. Please believe that.'

'I do.' But the brief hope this gave him was dashed when she added, 'You never gave a second thought to whether you hurt me or not. Or even a first thought.'

'Come into the dining room, everyone,' Hope called. 'Supper is served.'

He looked a question at her, but without much hope, and Luke appeared at her side. As they walked away together Primo remembered his mother describing how Luke had spoken of Olympia—'She's all mine.'

He'd been away in England for only a few days, yet it seemed that they were almost engaged. He tried to ignore the faint chill this thought caused him and put on a smile for the other guests.

A malign fate caused him to be seated directly opposite Olympia, where he had a grandstand view of her and Luke, laughing and talking over the meal, sometimes with their heads together. The candles on the table were reflected in her eyes and their glow seemed to pervade her whole being. How could he blame Luke for seeming entranced by her? He was entranced himself. He had never seen her look so beautiful, but it was not for him.

After the meal came dancing and every man there competed to dance with her. To Primo's rage they generally raised an eyebrow in Luke's direction in silent acknowledgement that she was 'his' woman. Grinning, Luke would give his permission, then watch her with fond, possessive eyes. Primo fully understood that feeling of possessiveness. It was the same one that made him want to knock his brother to the floor, throw Olympia over his shoulder and run away to hide in a cave, where no man's eyes but his own would ever see her.

'Glorious, isn't she?' said a voice at his elbow.

It was Luke, having made his way around the edge of the floor to join his brother.

'How did I ever hit so lucky?' he mused.

'How long have you known her?' Primo asked, trying to keep his voice neutral.

'Only since today.'

'Today?' He was startled.

'She sent me flying with her car. I haven't picked myself up yet. Maybe I never will. That's fine. When the moment happens, it happens.'

'Are you telling me,' Primo said in a carefully controlled voice, 'that after less than a day—?'

'Why not? Some women are so special that you know almost at once. Look at her. Isn't that a lady who could slay you in the first moment?'

'Don't be melodramatic,' Primo said harshly. His head was throbbing.

'Sure. I forgot you're the one man in the world who couldn't understand love at first sight. Take my word, it's the best.'

'Yes,' Primo murmured inaudibly. 'It is.'

'You knew her in England, didn't you?' Luke added. 'What's the story?'

'There is no story,' Primo said repressively.

'Odd that. She won't talk about you either.'

'Then mind your own damned business,' Primo said with soft venom.

'Like that, is it? Why don't you ask her to dance? It's cool with me.'

This time the look his brother turned on him was murderous. But the music was ending and Primo marched swiftly over to Olympia and reached for her hand, saying, 'Let's dance.'

'I think not,' she said. 'I've promised this one.'

She slid easily into the arms of an elderly uncle whose name she had forgotten but who beamed at his luck. Primo watched them, planning dire retribution on his innocent relative. It didn't help when the uncle's wife stood beside him, sighing happily. 'Isn't she a nice girl to be so kind to the old fool? It's not often he has such fun.'

When the dance was over Primo took no chances.

'The next one is with me,' he said, taking firm hold of her hand.

'I'd rather not, if you don't mind,' she said, trying to break free and failing.

The music was beginning. Primo's arm was about her waist in an unbreakable hold and Olympia found that she had no choice but to dance with him.

Such forcefulness was new, coming from him, and it increased her anger. Yet that very anger also seemed part of the heady excitement that the drama of the situation was causing to stream through her.

'Who the hell are you to be high-handed?' she demanded furiously.

He gave her a wolfish grin.

'I'm Primo Rinucci, a man I've heard you describe as ruthless and power-mad. A man to be hunted down by a determined woman and used for anything she can get out of him.'

'I never said that.'

'You said plenty that meant exactly that. So why should you be surprised if I act up to your picture of me?'

'All right, enjoy yourself while you can. Tomorrow I'm on the first plane home.'

'I think not. You have a contract with Leonate.'

'I never signed any contract.'

'You signed one with Curtis that has a year to run. Leonate own Curtis, which means that I own you for the next year.'

'The hell you do.'

'The hell I don't! What happens to you now is up to me. Leave now and I'll freeze you out of the entire industry, for good. You'll be amazed at how far my tentacles stretch. How's that for ruthless and power-mad?'

'About what I'd have expected.'

'Good, then we both know where we stand.'

'Let me go right now.'

'Not until you see sense,' he said harshly. 'I admit I behaved badly but I didn't plan it. It was mostly accident—'

'Oh, please,' she scoffed.

'It got out of hand, and when you've calmed down I'll explain—'

'You will not explain because I don't want to hear.'

'Olympia, please—'

'I said let me go'

Luke was watching Olympia and his brother with mixed feelings. He'd only known her a few hours, but already she affected him strongly. He'd been looking forward to knowing her better, and then better still. Even his mother's wild hopes hadn't seemed totally fanciful.

And now this!

For he couldn't kid himself. Primo's arrival had changed something drastically. If Olympia's face hadn't told him that, Primo's would have done. He'd seen emotions in his brother's face that he wouldn't have believed possible. He fixed brooding eyes on them and watched every detail.

When he saw Olympia wrench herself from Primo's grasp he went to her quickly.

'Why don't we slip away by ourselves?' he said. 'Mamma will forgive us.'

Hope's face confirmed it. When Luke signalled to her that he and Olympia were leaving she beamed and blew him a kiss, evidently convinced that the romance was proceeding perfectly.

'Olympia!' It was Primo, dark-faced with anger. 'You can't leave like this.'

'According to whom?' she demanded in outrage. 'Are you daring to give me orders? Just because you've had me dancing to your tune recently you think that's going to go on? Think again. It's over. Your cover's blown. Go on to the next victim and get out of my way.'

For a moment she thought he would refuse, he seemed so firmly set in her path. But then the tension seemed to go out of him and his eyes were suddenly bleak.

'Get out, then,' he said.

Taking Luke's arm, she hurried past him. She was suddenly afraid of Primo.

In half an hour they were seated in a small fish restaurant near the shore. Luke ordered spaghetti with clams and refused to let her speak until she had taken the first few mouthfuls.

She sighed with pleasure. 'Thank you. Now I feel so much better.'

'I had an ulterior motive,' he admitted. 'I expect to be rewarded with the whole story. What did the *bastardo* do?'

It would have been superfluous to ask who the *bastardo* was.

When she didn't reply, he said gently, 'You did know him, didn't you?'

'Yes, we met in England.'

'But he didn't tell you he was Primo Rinucci?'

'No, he said he was Jack Cayman.'

Luke gave a soft whistle.

'The devil he did! Well, it was his father's name.'

'Yes, your mother told me. She says he's Italian on his mother's side.'

'We're never too sure how much of him is English and how much Italian, and I doubt if he knows either. He sometimes uses the name Cayman in business—'

'This wasn't business,' she said in a tense voice.

He didn't press her any further, but gradually she found it easier to talk. By the time they had finished the spaghetti and had passed on to the oven-baked mullet Luke had a hazy idea of what had happened. Not that she told him many details, but he was good at interpreting the silences.

He was astounded. Primo had done this? His brother, whose name was a byword for good sense, upright behaviour and totally boring probity, had not only lived a double life, but had managed to conduct a clandestine liaison with his own lover. For how else could it be described?

In fact Primo had behaved disgracefully.

Luke was proud of him!

'All I want to do now is go back to England and never see or hear his name again,' she said bitterly. 'But I've signed a contract and he says he'll hold me to it.'

'But of course you're not going home,' Luke said at once. 'You're going to stay here and make him sorry.'

She looked at him, suddenly alert.

'You're right,' she said. 'That's a much better way. Of course it is. I just couldn't bear the thought that he'd been having a big laugh at my expense.'

'But you had a laugh at his expense tonight. Did you see his face when he realised it was you? He looked as if he'd swallowed a hedgehog.'

'Yes, he did,' she mused as the moment came back to her, the details clearer now than they'd been at the time.

'There are going to be other moments like that, plenty of them, because you're going to get your revenge and I'm going to help you do it.'

She smiled at him.

'How?' she asked.

'I'll tell you.'

CHAPTER NINE

PRIMO stayed at the party as long as he could endure it, partly for his mother's sake and partly because he was afraid of what he might do if he followed Luke and Olympia. In the early hours he departed and drove around the city disconsolately until at last he turned the car to the place he had always intended to go.

As he drew up outside the Vallini he saw that the lights of her suite were still on. So she hadn't carried out her threat to leave. He let out a long breath of relief, discovering that his whole body was aching with tension.

The young man on the desk smiled, recognising him from a few days earlier. 'I'll just let her know.'

But Primo stopped him reaching for the phone. 'I want to surprise her.'

'I'm really supposed to call ahead, *signore*.'

A note changed hands.

'I guess you forgot,' Primo said with a conspiratorial smile.

'*Si, signore.*'

She took so long to answer the door that he wondered if she'd left after all. But at last she opened it. Her face set when she saw him but he was ready for this and put his foot in the door before she could slam it. With a swift movement he was inside, facing her fury.

'Get out of here!' she flashed.

'Not until we've had a talk.'

'We've had it. It's over.'

'You didn't let me say anything.'

'I let you say all that I was interested in hearing. Which was zilch. Just what do you imagine there is to say? I trusted you and all the time you were setting me up. I don't know what pleasure you got out of it, but whatever it was you should be ashamed.'

'I am. I never meant it to go so far. Please, Olympia, it was just a joke that got out of hand.'

'You kept it going a lot longer than that.'

'Things happened unexpectedly. It all ran out of control.'

'I don't believe what I'm hearing. It ran out of your control? Primo Rinucci, the big boss, the man in charge, who snaps his fingers and people jump—'

'Cut that out,' he raged. 'You created a tailor's dummy and told yourself a load of stories about him, but he's not me. He never was.'

'Why didn't you stop me?'

'Because I was enjoying myself,' he said rashly.

'Ah, now we have it. You loved making a fool of me—'

'I didn't mean that. I meant—'

Somewhere there were the words that would tell her of the delight he'd known during those few days when he'd teased and incited her while falling under her spell. There must be words for the sweetness that had engulfed him, the sense of a miracle, so long awaited, that must be treated with care, lest it vanish. And more words for the fear that overcame him whenever he thought of telling the truth and risking everything.

Yes, there were words. If only he could find them.

'Well?' she demanded remorselessly.

'I didn't mean it to turn out the way it did,' was the best he could manage.

'No, you didn't mean to get caught out.'

'That wasn't what I—'

'Just how did you plan to tell me? Or didn't you?'

'Of course I was going to tell you, but it was hard. I knew you'd misunderstand.'

'Surely not?' she said caustically. 'How could anyone misunderstand a man who gives a false name and lures a woman into making a fool of herself just so that he can have a cheap laugh? Men do it every day, and women put up with it.'

'And what about what women do every day?' he demanded, stung to anger. 'You were planning a good laugh yourself, weren't you? When Rinucci turned up you were going to take him for a ride. You had it all worked out, down to the last detail, fluttering your eyelashes, plus the old hair trick culled from a hundred corny films.

'You even enlisted me to give you ''inside information''—your own words—to weaken his defences, and never mind what a fool you'd be making of him when he turned up and I watched you bringing him down. I may have behaved badly, but that's nothing to the derision you piled on him—I mean me. Oh, hell!'

'You can't even sort out which of you is which,' she snapped.

'That's true,' he said wryly.

'What do you think it was like for me to find out the truth the way I did?'

'How could I have anticipated that? I didn't know you were going to be at my mother's.'

'I wouldn't have been if I'd known you were coming back. You kept very quiet about it.'

'I wanted to surprise you.'

'You sure as hell did that.'

'Olympia, please, I know I did wrong, but it wasn't for a laugh.'

'You'll never get me to believe that in a million years, so don't try.'

She turned and stormed away from him. She'd changed out of her glamorous red dress into serviceable trousers and sweater. Her face was free of make-up and her hair was dishevelled. It looked as if she'd torn down the elaborate arrangement then scragged it back any old how. A few wisps hung down over her face, softening the austere lines.

Despite her rage it was her misery that reached him most poignantly. Without the glitz she was pale and slightly wan, and even more beautiful in his eyes. He longed to reach out to her but he knew it wasn't the right time. She wasn't ready to hear what he had to say.

She was walking up and down the room now, brooding bitterly. 'All those things I said. I trusted you.'

The injustice of this made his temper rise again.

'Yes, you trusted me with a blow-by-blow account of the unscrupulous methods a woman adopts to bring a man to heel. A real eye-opener! I should write a book about it. Men beware! This is what they get up to. You turned me into a fellow conspirator with myself as the intended victim. I don't know who to feel sorrier for—me or me!'

'I warned you I wasn't a nice person,' she told him. 'Remember that day I said that I was up front about what I wanted and what I'd do to get it? You should have believed me.'

'I did believe you,' he shouted. 'How could I not when I was getting a demonstration every moment? You did a great job. Up front with *me,* not with him, although of course you couldn't have afforded to be. That's what you're really angry about, isn't it? You showed your weapons to the wrong man and now they're dead in your hands.'

'Don't worry, I'm not planning to use them on you.'

'But you *did* use them on me, and to hell with me and my feelings! Did you ever think of your victim? Suppose I'd fallen in love with you?'

'Be honest! You were in no danger of that.'

'Luckily for me I wasn't. I'm safe against your kind—'

'And just what is my "kind"?'

'Heartless, scheming, manipulative, calculating—take your pick. Yes, I'm safe, but you didn't know that. If I'd fallen in love with you that wouldn't have mattered, would it? Just a casualty of the war, only it wasn't my war, you heartless woman!'

In despair she stared at him. All the things that had seemed so simple before, when she had prided herself on being immune to feelings, now presented themselves in stark, livid colours, shocking in the light he turned on them.

When she spoke her voice shook. 'Then it's fortunate for both of us that you're so armoured—almost as armoured as I am.'

'Yes, I noticed that,' he said softly. 'When I held you, trembling in my arms, I thought how cold and indifferent you were.'

Her eyes glittered in a way he knew. 'I do it very well, don't I?' she said softly. 'I know all the right buttons to press, and I can press them in the right order.'

He paled. 'Are you telling me it was all an act?'

'Are you so sure it wasn't?'

Her words brought them to the edge of the precipice, showing him the disaster waiting below.

'Olympia, don't,' he said urgently. 'Don't do this, please don't, for both our sakes.'

'But what do you think I'm doing? Just being honest, that's all.'

'This isn't honesty. It's pride and revenge, and maybe you have the right, but don't do it. Don't ruin what we still might have.'

She gave a cruel laugh. 'You actually imagine that there might be something between us, after this?'

'I know it sounds crazy, but that's because we've been performing in masks, inventing other selves and thinking that's who we were. But if we could get clear of that and be ourselves—'

He left the implication hanging in the air and for a moment he thought he'd won. Her face softened and a weary look passed across it. But then she said, 'If we could do that we'd probably find we liked each other—and ourselves—even less. It's too late, Ja—' She broke off and a spasm of pain went over her face. 'Signor Rinucci.'

'Don't call me that,' he shouted.

'It's a useful reminder, in case I forget,' she cried back at him. 'Or in case you do.'

He closed his eyes. His world was disintegrating about him and whatever he did made it worse. He could only say her name in anguish.

'Olympia—Olympia—'

'*Don't.*'

They stood in silence, neither knowing what to say.

He looked around him and suddenly noticed things that he'd failed to notice before, and which now seemed ominous.

A half-packed suitcase stood open on the sofa and several clothes were draped over the back.

'Packing?' he breathed. 'Now?'

'Yes, now. I'm moving out of here tonight.'

'I told you, you can't go back to England.'

'I'm not. I've decided to stay and take up the job with Leonate. But I'm moving out of here tonight and going where you can't follow me.'

'There's nowhere I can't follow you, and I will.'

'You don't need to. I'm coming to work to-morrow. Or is that another of your fictions?'

'No, the job is there.'

'Then it's about time I met my colleagues, Signore Leonate and Signor Rinucci who, I understand, is the real power behind the throne. I'm longing to meet *him*—that is, if you can sort out which one he is.'

'Stop it,' he said violently. 'Are you going to beat me over the head with that for ever?'

'I can try.'

'So you reckon you're the injured innocent? I don't think so. I may have laid a small trap, but you made it bigger and jumped in with both feet. I'm sorry you feel foolish, but it's nothing to the kind of foolish that I'd have felt if things had worked out the way you meant.'

He came closer to her, seizing her arm so that she couldn't turn away from him.

'That was quite a plan you had, Olympia. Rinucci was going to turn up and you were going to use your wiles on him, and I was going to do what, exactly? Cheer you on from the sidelines? Suppose I'd warned him and brought your house of cards tumbling down? Did you think of that? Of course you didn't, because you never thought that far ahead.'

'How far ahead did you think?' she flung at him.

'Not far enough, which is why I don't blame you too much—'

'Big of you, considering that you started it.'

'That's arguable. You said a lot of things before you made the most cursory check who

I was. The astute operator you want me to believe in wouldn't have done that. Perhaps I should question your skills a little more. Not your seductive skills, because we know about those—'

There was a crack as her hand connected with his face. Then something seemed to hold them both petrified. Her eyes were filled with anger, bitterness and insult. But there was also anguish and a kind of fear.

He saw it and his own anger died. Even at this moment he discovered that he couldn't bear to see her hurt. It made quarrelling very difficult.

'Let's say that makes us even,' he told her quietly. 'Now can we draw a line under it?'

'I don't know,' she said in a choking voice.

'But I do.' He turned her towards him and gently drew her close. 'That's it,' he said as he lowered his mouth to hers. 'No more fighting. It's finished.'

'You can't just—'

'Yes, I can,' he said, silencing her.

The last thought of which she was capable was, *How dare he?*

How dared he think that one kiss could make up for everything, and that she would simply do as he asked because his lips thrilled her? She would show him that he was wrong— she *must* show him that—just as soon as her strength came back.

But instead of returning it was draining away with every movement of his mouth against hers, as her body grew warmer, more eager to be his, and with less will of its own.

'The past is over,' he murmured against her mouth. 'It's the future that matters.'

'But how can we—?' she whispered back.

'I don't know. Who knows the future? We make it ourselves. Hold me.'

She did so, sliding her arms about his neck, part embracing him, part clinging to him for safety. There were no thoughts now, only the blind instinct to seek him, join with him, belong to him.

The past no longer mattered. She'd known she was falling in love with him. She'd faced it, accepted it, even welcomed it. Now she felt the warmth of his body communicating itself to hers and she knew that she needed that warmth, not only in her flesh but in her heart.

For too many years she'd been cold, hiding from love in her bleak cave. She knew now that only he could tempt her out. It was a risk, but every skilled movement of his mouth, his hands, urged her to take that risk and say, with him, that the past was over and they would make the future together.

In a haze of delight she was barely aware of him moving, drawing her after him in the direction of her bedroom. Not until she heard the door click did she get a sense of danger.

'Wait—' she said urgently.

He picked her up in his arms. 'Haven't we waited long enough?'

'But there's something I must—you don't understand—'

'I understand this,' he said, kissing her again. 'What else is there to understand?'

As he spoke he kicked the door open and walked into the grandiose bedroom, heading for the huge luxurious bed, so absorbed in his passion that he was close up to it before he realised that something was there that shouldn't have been.

A man was stretched out on the coverlet, his hands behind his head, grinning derisively.

'Hallo,' said Luke.

For a moment Primo could do no more than stare at his brother. Just as Olympia, earlier that evening, had told herself that what she saw was impossible, so now Primo closed, opened and closed his eyes, certain that the next time Luke would have disappeared.

But he stayed there, solid and, to his brother, thoroughly objectionable.

'You really should have warned me,' Primo said, speaking to Olympia but not looking at her. 'But if I'd been sharper I'd have expected it.'

'Will you please put me down?' she said edgily.

He meant to lower her with dignity but shock was causing the strength to drain away from his arms. They gave way abruptly and she ended up sprawling on the bed where Luke quickly took hold of her to stop her sliding off.

'No need to throw the lady about,' Luke observed. 'Not that I mind, you understand.'

Primo treated this remark with disdain. It was that or murder.

'What a picture!' he said softly. 'I should have known, shouldn't I?'

'How dare you?' Olympia flashed. 'Luke came here to help me to get out of this place.'

She scrambled to the floor, flushed and panting. Torn by conflicting feelings, bitterness and passion, she felt she would explode any minute. For a blinding moment she hated both of them.

'If you're thinking what I think you are—' she threw at Primo.

'He was waiting for you in your bedroom all the time,' he said with a thin smile. 'What do you expect me to think?'

'He's fully dressed, or haven't you noticed that? I told you, Luke came here to help me.'

'Hidden in your bedroom?' Primo demanded, almost savagely. The thought that Luke had been here all the time, listening, made him wild.

'That's where people usually do their packing,' Luke pointed out, indicating another open suitcase. 'I've just been fetching and carrying, acting like a maid.'

'Helping your mistress undress?' Primo asked coldly. 'Isn't that what a maid does?'

'Among other things.'

'Shut up both of you,' Olympia said fiercely. 'You—' she turned on Primo '—you do not own me, you do not give me orders, I am not answerable to you, except at work.'

'Where I expect you to be tomorrow morning,' he snapped. 'Be on time.'

'He's right, we'd better be going,' Luke said, scrambling off the bed. 'Olympia, I'll wait for you in the next room.'

'There's no need, I'm coming,' she said. 'Everything's packed.'

She began to close the suitcase, not looking at Primo. He watched her in silence for a moment.

At last he spoke in a harsh voice. 'Will you tell me where you're going to stay? Or needn't I ask?'

Now she looked at him and was startled by his face. She had seen him charming, and sometimes annoyed, but never coldly venomous, as now. Beneath the surface control he was in a bitter rage that threatened to engulf him, and for the second time that night she was actually afraid of him.

'You needn't ask,' she said. 'I'm staying in Luke's apartment.'

'Then get out of my sight and don't talk to me again,' he raged. '*Go on! Get out!*'

Since her car was still at the hotel, Luke took her to work the next morning and introduced her to Enrico Leonate. He was a plump elderly man with a genial manner and he welcomed her with open arms.

'Primo has told me so much about you,' he enthused.

'I hope he's explained that my Italian is very basic,' Olympia said.

'It will improve, and in the meantime we all speak English very well.'

'And besides, Miss Lincoln is a quick learner,' said a voice behind her.

'Ah, Primo,' Enrico cried. 'Come in. Miss Lincoln and I were just introducing ourselves.'

'Please call me Olympia,' she said to the old man.

'Then you must call me Enrico. Primo, here she is, and just as lovely as you said.'

'I don't think I said that exactly,' Primo replied coolly.

'But you—'

'Described her as businesslike, focused, intelligent, diligent and—as I said before, a very quick learner. She's particularly good at winning people over.'

'That's what we need,' Enrico roared happily.

'Don't accept everything Signor Rinucci says about me,' Olympia said lightly. 'He's prejudiced.'

'Of course he's prejudiced in your favour. He saw you at work in England.'

'That's very true,' Primo murmured.

'And you were impressed?'

'Oh, yes, it was an impressive sight. I believe I've said as much to you since, *signorina*.'

'You have indeed,' she riposted. 'But I was learning much from you, a true master in the art of manipulation.'

'That's his Italian side,' Enrico said triumphantly. 'It is our gift to see things from many angles at once. When you have been with us for a while, you too will have learned it. Primo will teach you.'

'You do the *signorina* an injustice,' Primo said. 'She has nothing to learn from me.'

Luke had been watching this exchange from where he'd been standing quietly by the window, his eyes alight with malicious pleasure. Now, as though feeling that he'd enjoyed the entertainment long enough, he roused himself to say, 'I'd better be going. Call me later, Olympia, and I'll collect you.'

'I don't want to be a nuisance,' she said. 'I could get my car from the Vallini and drive home.'

'You don't know the way yet. It was dark when we did the journey last night.' He gave her a warm smile. 'And how could you ever be a nuisance?'

'That's a very nice thing to say, but actually it's just a slur on my driving.'

'I was maintaining a diplomatic silence about your driving,' he said with a grin.

'Goodbye!' she told him firmly.

'Yes, goodbye,' Primo said without looking up.

Luke winked at Olympia and departed.

'Primo has told me how you took him around the Curtis factories,' Enrico said. 'Now I think he should return the favour and show you around the Leonate empire.'

'Actually, Enrico, that's a bit difficult,' Primo said. 'I've got a backlog of work to get through. I suggest that Signora Pattino undertakes this task.'

'As you say. Well, why don't you show Olympia to her office?'

'No, you do that. I have to get going. *Signorina*, I should like to welcome you to Leonate and hope that you will be happy with us.'

He said the last words like a robot and was gone instantly.

'Well, he really does have a lot to do,' Enrico said, sounding awkward. 'Let's go.'

That day was like the culmination of every ambitious dream she'd ever had. The office he showed her was modern, attractive and better than her old one. They discussed the firm and he was impressed with her knowledge.

'You've been learning about Leonate,' he said. 'Well done! You're everything Primo said you'd be.'

He swept her off to lunch, taking also Signora Pattino, his Personal Assistant, a comfortable, middle-aged woman who said she would enjoy being her guide in the coming days. Wherever she went she was welcomed as an asset by people who knew nothing about her except what Primo had told them.

But whatever he'd said was in the past. This morning he'd shown a cruel irony that reflected his true feelings now. Their conversation, superficially friendly, had been charged with hidden meaning that Enrico hadn't understood.

But Luke had understood every word.

CHAPTER TEN

PRIMO, descending into Leonate's underground car park prior to departure, saw his brother just drawing up and noticed sourly that he had a flashy new car. Which explained, he thought, why he hadn't recognised it outside the hotel the night before.

Luke got out of the car and hailed him cheerfully. 'Is she ready and waiting for me?'

'Since I haven't seen *Signorina* Lincoln all afternoon, I couldn't tell you,' Primo said frostily.

'Very formal suddenly. I expect that was her idea, and it's no more than you deserve. Did nobody ever explain to you that it's customary to introduce yourself to the lady at the start? With the right name, I mean. It does wonders for putting them in a good mood.'

'*She told you?*'

Luke shrugged. 'I hardly needed telling. At the party last night, it became very obvious what you'd done.'

'And I suppose you jumped at the chance to serve me an ill turn,' Primo raged. 'Something you've been waiting to do.'

'Don't blame me. I'm innocent in all this.'

'Am I supposed to believe it was an accident that she was at the villa?'

'Of course it was. Don't be a damned fool! It was bound to happen sooner or later. You shouldn't have left her alone.'

'I only meant to be away for a day,' Primo said through gritted teeth. 'Things proved to be more complicated when I got there.'

'Things always do. What happened to the man who planned everything and took no chances?'

Primo glared at him with sombre resentment. He could have said that this man had died the moment he'd set eyes on Olympia, replaced by another who would take any wild risk to claim her. But hell would freeze over before he said this to his brother and enemy.

'You're really enjoying this, aren't you?' he snapped.

'The situation has its charm. Serves you right for playing such a tomfool trick! You're usually such a stick-in-the-mud. Not last night, though. If there's one man I'd never have expected to pick the lady up and carry her to bed, it's you. Pity I was there to spoil the fun.'

The last word was choked off as Luke found himself thrust back against the wall with his brother's hand at his throat.

'One more word and I won't be responsible for my actions,' Primo said murderously.

'Hey, calm down. All right, let's leave it.'

Primo released him, leaving Luke to rub his throat and take deep breaths.

'Another side of you I never suspected,' he said, slightly hoarsely. 'Well, well.'

'I'm warning you, Luke, she's not for you.'

'Isn't that for her to decide?'

'*Stay away from her.*'

'That would be hard since we're living together.'

'Don't fool yourself. She only went with you to revenge herself on me. She cares nothing for you.'

'You're sure of that, are you?' His eyes met Primo's in a direct challenge.

'Go to hell,' Primo said.

'If I can take her with me, I'll go anywhere. Ah, here she is.'

Luke went forward to greet Olympia with a kiss on the cheek, but Primo did not see this. He walked away to his own car, got in and drove away.

As Luke drove her home he asked, 'Did he give you a hard time today, demanding explanations and so forth?'

'Not at all. He barely spoke to me.'

'Good. Don't you go explaining anything. It's no business of his.'

'I know. It's just that it feels like deceiving him.'

'Not deceiving. Just leading him up the garden path. And let's face it, that's how you two communicate.'

She gave a wry laugh. 'That's true enough.'

Luke's home was on the southern boundary of Naples, in a recently built apartment block. Here everything was ultra-modern and shining. The computer was the latest, smoothest, most powerful of its kind. So was the internet connection, the printer, and 'all the other bells and whistles' as Luke cynically put it.

The same was true of everything in the kitchen, where the cooking arrangements were so complex that they could have propelled a spacecraft to the moon.

'But they also do a mean scrambled egg,' Luke had pointed out the previous night, then proceeded to demonstrate.

The apartment had two bedrooms, both with double beds and acres of wardrobe space. Her suitcases were still only half unpacked in the guest room, and now she hung up the rest of her things.

Luke knocked on the door. 'I've made you some tea.'

'Thank you,' she said fervently.

While they were drinking tea she said, 'I'd offer to cook supper but I don't think I could cope with your kitchen.'

'Another time. You have a lot of reading to do, if that stuff you've brought home means anything.'

'Right, and I'm going to have to work hard because it's in Italian and I'm still learning.'

'Let me know if you need any help.'

She studied while he cooked, refusing to let her help. Nor would he allow her to help clear away after the excellent meal. After several hours devoted to files, with his assistance over awkward words, she felt she was beginning to get a grip on things.

How would it have felt if it had been Primo here, helping her out, caring for her with kindness? She closed her eyes. He no longer existed.

By the end of the evening she had a strange sense of contentment and safety. Luke even made her a mug of cocoa and said goodnight to her at her bedroom door.

She didn't see Primo for two days and then he dropped into her office without warning.

'Getting ready to go?' he asked, seeing her tidying papers on her desk.

'Yes, Signora Pattino and I are setting out tomorrow. I'm looking forward to it.'

She tried to speak normally, not letting him see how the sight of him affected her.

'Good. Enrico tells me that you're doing well.'

'He seems to have started with a good opinion of me. That must be down to you.'

'I told him what I thought, that your executive talents are considerable.'

'Even though you hate me?'

'I don't hate you, Olympia, and I hope you don't hate me. You did what you had to do. I should have understood sooner. It would have saved us both a lot of pain.'

The pain was there in his face. She saw it when she looked up, and her heart went out to him.

But he didn't want her heart. He was still unyielding. Nothing in him was reaching out to her in return.

'Are you talking about Luke?' she asked.

'It hardly matters now.'

'Don't wave me aside like that. Of course it matters.'

'I just think you might have warned me that he was in your bedroom.'

'I told him to stay out of sight while I got rid of you. I meant to do that in ten seconds.'

'But you didn't—'

'I got angry with you and I forgot about him. He was only helping me pack—'

'And undress.'

'It was a hired dress. I had to leave it behind. I changed into something plain and useful, as you saw.' She folded her arms and gave him a challenging look. 'I promise you, they were not my seduction clothes.'

'True. I remember.'

'I've got to get going.' She turned away to her desk but he detained her with a hand on her arm.

'I just want you to know—I really didn't throw you down on to the bed. It was an accident.'

She gave a shaky laugh. 'I guess I knew that. You're not the caveman type—whichever one of you was there that night.' She saw him close his eyes suddenly. 'Hey, I was only joking. It's the past. Over and done with.'

'As you say, over and done with. But I wish you weren't living with Luke.'

'Maybe I'll find somewhere else later, when I know more about Naples.'

'I've got friends in the business. I could—'

'Primo, stop this. You can't organise me. Not everyone can be bought off with a hefty tip.'

'What do you mean?'

'I mean the hotel receptionist who didn't call ahead to warn me you were coming. He was apologetic when I went down. He didn't actually say you bribed him, but I guess you have your own methods of persuasion. Primo Rinucci always gets his own way, doesn't he?'

'Not always,' he said sadly. 'Sometimes even he knows when he has to admit defeat. Goodbye, *Signorina* Lincoln. I wish you well in your career.'

The soft touch of his lips on her cheek was unnerving. Then he was gone.

She and Signora Pattino were away for a week touring the Leonate factories in southern Italy. They got on well; Olympia drank in information about the firm and her companion was impressed.

Everything she had ever wanted would soon be hers, but now she wanted something more. And she had lost it.

But as they began the long drive back her courage revived. She was haunted by the memory of their last meeting, the sadness she had sensed in him despite his distant manner. He wasn't cold to her, whatever he might want her to believe. Sometimes she could still feel his kiss on her cheek.

They were working in the same building. She would have a hundred chances to take him aside, persuade him to talk. And out of that talk would come understanding and mutual forgiveness.

Surely it was the same with him. The time apart had allowed their tempers to cool and now they were ready to move on. The future could still be theirs. As she arrived back in Naples she was full of confidence and almost happiness.

Enrico welcomed her back jubilantly, and in Italian.

'Such glowing reports I've had of you! Everyone says you're wonderful.'

'Everyone's been very kind to me,' she said, also in Italian.

'Ah, Primo was right to praise you. If only he could be here to see your triumph. But I'll tell him next time I phone England.'

'England?'

'Yes, he had to go back. Cedric Tandy's confidence has been shaken by the Banyon episode, and he says he can't go on. So Primo's had to dash back and take over until a full-time replacement will be found. He'll be away for quite a while.'

Olympia often thought that Primo would have been surprised if he could have seen her at home with Luke, who acted like a kindly brother. Since he had an arrangement with a firm who cleaned the place and took care of his laundry she had nothing to do but think of her career.

Sometimes he would take her to the villa to have dinner with the family. Hope would overwhelm her with tender consideration, clearly trying to smooth their 'romance' along, which made Olympia feel slightly awkward but Luke seemed unperturbed.

Once, while she was there, the phone rang. Hope answered it, saying, '*Ciao, caro,*' and it soon became clear that she was talking to Primo. Olympia listened to the flood of Italian which was too rapid for her to follow in detail, but she could tell that there was no mention of him returning home soon.

Hope hung up with a sigh. 'I like to have them around me,' she said. 'I am unreasonable, since they are all grown men, but there!

Mothers *are* unreasonable. And perhaps it's better for Primo and Luke to be apart just now.'

There was a slight buzzing in Olympia's ears. 'Why just now?' she asked, trying not to sound too curious.

'It's hard to say. All their lives they have been fighting. If it's not about this, it's about that. The last thing was a man they both wanted to employ, but Primo snatched him from under Luke's nose. ''Stole him'' according to Luke. But that's not important. There's something else, something that causes really bad blood between them.'

It gave Olympia a shock to realise that Hope still didn't know what had been between herself and Primo. She thought they had met for the first time at the party.

'Was that Primo?' Luke asked from the doorway.

'Yes, he is well and he sends his love to everyone.'

'Including me?' Luke asked in disbelief.

'Including you,' Hope said firmly.

'Perhaps I'd better test it for poison first.'

'Stop that,' Hope ordered him, suddenly stern. 'Whatever it is that has come between you, he is still your brother.'

'Sorry, Mamma,' Luke said sheepishly. He put his arms about her and kissed her. 'It's nothing,' he told her tenderly. 'You know that he and I have always been at odds about one thing or another.'

'But this time it's serious, I know it is. Why won't you tell me?'

'Because it's nothing. Come on, you know what we're like. If we're not scrapping we're not happy.'

After that he exerted himself to make her laugh and the matter was allowed to pass.

Primo wasn't mentioned again, but he stayed in Olympia's thoughts and perhaps Luke's too, because he suddenly began talking about him as they drove home that night.

'He's a contradictory man in many ways,' he mused. 'He can feel something with all his being, while doing things that go completely in the other direction.'

'Surely most people can do that?'

'Yes, but he takes it to extremes. Maybe it's the result of not really knowing whether he's

Italian or English. You only have to look at how he behaved over our brother Justin.'

'Exactly who is Justin?' she asked curiously. 'I keep hearing odd bits of information but never very much. He's almost like a ghost.'

'For years he was a completely taboo subject. We all knew that Mamma had another son, but nobody knew what had happened to him. She was only fifteen when she became pregnant. She wasn't married, of course, and in those days it was a great stigma. What her parents did was unforgivable, but they must have been desperate.'

'What did they do?'

'Snatched her baby, handed it over for adoption and told her he'd been born dead.'

'Dear God!' Olympia exclaimed, shocked to the core.

'She never got over the loss of her baby. She married Jack Cayman and became Primo's stepmother. Primo couldn't remember his real mother and he adored Hope from the start. When they adopted me he wasn't best pleased. I was competition for her attention, you see. We've always fought and bickered.

'But I think the thing that really got to him, almost as much as it did Hope, was when she discovered that her baby hadn't died after all. She went crazy trying to find him, but it was too late. He'd been adopted. She'd lost him.

'Her marriage didn't last. When it ended she took me with her, but Primo was Jack's son and she couldn't claim custody. But when Jack died Primo's Italian family brought him here and she contacted him again. Since she married Toni we've all been one big family.

'But Mamma never forgot her first son. She couldn't trace him, but when he turned eighteen she began hoping that he would try to trace her. No luck though.

'In the end it was Primo who found him. He contacted every private eye in England that he could find, putting down markers, saying he was to be notified if anyone likely turned up. And in the end it happened.

'But here's the strange thing. Primo was always jealous of Justin for displacing him as Mamma's eldest son. Yet he did it for her, because he knew what it meant to her. It took him fifteen years, and, when he got the first hint, he went over to England to meet him, check him out, then bring him back here.'

'What a wonderful thing for him to do,' Olympia said, touched.

'Yes, it was. My brother drives me nuts sometimes. He's pig-headed, too sure of himself, blinkered, obstinate—but then he'll do something that makes you stare, and wonder if you could be as generous as that. And I don't think most people could.'

His words brought back a memory—Primo talking on the phone to an agitated Cedric, calming him with kindness, promising to be there for him, no matter the inconvenience.

And that was the real Primo, the one who could empathise with someone else, even when it was against his own interests.

'Fifteen years,' she murmured. 'He would have been so young when he started.'

'True. Fifteen years of patient watching and waiting. That's very Primo. He knows how to take his time. Incredibly, he's still jealous. Mamma's thrilled about what he did for her. She calls him her hero. But he minds about Justin because he feels displaced.'

His words gave Olympia a strange feeling because they cast a new light on Primo's behaviour in England: watching and waiting, moving slowly towards his goal, keeping in the shadows while she tricked and teased another man—even though that man was himself.

She thought of the quiet, self-effacing generosity of someone who would spend years seeking a person he didn't really want to find, to please the mother he loved.

How she wished she could have known him under other circumstances! How different things might have been!

Life with Luke was contented. She found him easy to talk to and he soon knew all about her, including the story of her elderly parents. After an initial hesitation she told him about the Valentine cards and how she'd fooled Primo.

'So he was living with you?' Luke asked when he'd finished laughing.

'No, he just stayed one night.'

'Ah, I see.'

'No, you don't see,' she said, aiming a swipe at him. 'It was because he had a bump on the head.'

'Which you gave him?'

'In a manner of speaking. We had a little altercation on the way home and he crashed his car into mine.'

He eyed her askance. 'None of the men in my family are safe from you in a car, are they?'

'Anyway, Valentine's was next day and you should have seen his face when the cards arrived. And the red roses that my parents always send me.'

'Have they ever been to Naples?' he asked.

'Never. I took them to Paris once as a treat, but apart from that they've never been abroad.'

'I'm going to be away for a few days. Why not invite them to stay here?'

'You really mean that?'

'Why not? Give them a real vacation. They'll enjoy the *Maggio dei Monumenti*.'

'Whatever's that?'

'Literally it means May of the Monuments, although it starts in the last week in April. For a few weeks many museums and monuments open for free, and because they attract such crowds other things have started up at the same time—fairs, dance spectacles, that sort of thing.'

'Wait, I saw a puppet show in the street yesterday,' she remembered.

'That's right, it's just started, and now there'll be processions and concerts of Neapolitan songs. Spring is coming and it's a great way to celebrate. Call your parents and get them down for the fun.'

She did so, booked and paid for the tickets, and met them at the airport three days later. It was a joyous reunion, only slightly marred by her mother's immediate exclamation, 'Darling, you look so thin and tired. Are you working too hard?'

They behaved, as she afterwards told Luke, 'like a couple of kids at the seaside for the first time.' She spent the weekend showing them around the city, now growing warmer as April passed into May. When she had to return to work they were sufficiently confident to make their own way around, and even to take a day trip to Pompeii to see the ruins.

The following evening Enrico took them all out to dinner, entertained them with outrageous stories and flirted like mad with

Olympia's mother, while her father looked on in resignation.

'She's incorrigible,' he told his daughter. 'She always has been.' But he said it with a touch of pride.

They returned home to the disconcerting sight of Luke, asleep on the sofa.

'I got back early,' he said, getting up and rubbing his eyes. 'My business finished quickly, and I wanted to meet our guests.'

They were charmed by him, especially since he put himself out to achieve that very object. They all sat up late into the night eating pizzas, drinking wine and becoming the best of friends. By the time they'd finished he was calling them Harold and Angela.

There was an awkward moment when it became clear that Luke meant to spend the night on the sofa.

'Oh, but there's no need for that,' said Angela, anxious to be broad-minded. 'I mean—just because we're here there's no need for you to do anything different—'

'Let it go,' Harold begged, covering his eyes.

'But I only—'

'Darling, they know their own business best. Come to bed. Goodnight, you two.'

He said the last words hastily and almost carried his wife out of the room.

When they had gone Luke regarded her gleefully. 'I think I've just been given your mother's permission to—'

'Yes, I know what she's given you permission *to*—' she said with heavy irony. 'Thank you for being nice to my parents. Now, I think I'll go to bed.'

'Are you sure you don't want me to come with you? Since it's all right with your mother—'

'Luke, I'm warning you—'

'All right. It was worth a try.' He gave a melancholy sigh. 'Back to the sofa.'

'Goodnight.' She was laughing.

He grinned. 'Goodnight.'

Next morning his mutual admiration society with Angela was increased when, owing to a failure in communication, she walked into the bathroom while he was in the shower. Retreating in haste, she confided to her daughter, 'He's got ever such nice legs, dear.'

'*Mum!* Does your husband know that you notice men's legs?'

'Only too well,' Harold moaned. 'I can't take her on the beach.'

She regarded them fondly. They had been married for fifty years and they were like a pair of crazy, loving children. This was how marriage should be, and how it so seldom was.

They've found a secret that I'll never find, she thought. *If I'd known, I might never have lost him.*

CHAPTER ELEVEN

OVER breakfast Luke called his mother, then announced that he was taking them all to the villa that night. Her parents exchanged looks and Olympia realised with dismay that this had given another twist to the screw of her supposed love affair with Luke.

But it was hard to deny it right now when she was still sore from Primo's behaviour. At least Luke was saving her face, which perhaps was his kindly intention. Living together was possible because his manner towards her was never loverlike.

Then she put the thought aside to concentrate on making her parents' visit memorable. They were guests of honour at the villa, treated like royalty, with the whole family lined up on the steps to greet them.

Toni kissed Angela's hand, followed by Francesco, then Carlo, then Ruggiero, then—

'Look who's here,' Hope said excitedly to Olympia. 'But I expect you already knew.'

'No, I didn't know Primo was back,' she said, trying to catch her breath.

She felt her hand taken into his, the shock of his warmth and strength. She was struggling to clear her head.

'I haven't contacted Enrico yet,' he said. 'But when I called home and Mamma said we had honoured guests, of course I had to be here.'

'Of course,' she murmured.

It was six weeks since she'd seen him, and he'd changed. His hair had lost its slightly shaggy look and was trimmed back neat and severe against his skull. It made him look older and slightly stern. Then she realised that the real change was in his face. He had lost weight and there were shadows under his eyes, which seemed darker, yet more brilliant.

Olympia suddenly remembered her mother's remarks about her own looks. So he too had lain awake through long, lonely nights, thinking of how different things might have been.

He greeted Angela and Harold with perfect courtesy, but with a slight reserve that afterwards made Angela whisper to her daughter, 'I don't like him as much as his brother.'

Hope swept the two elderly people away for a glass of wine. Primo surveyed Luke, standing just behind Olympia.

'Allow me to congratulate you,' he said, 'on your engagement.'

Olympia made a helpless gesture. 'Primo—look—'

She was about to say that there was no engagement, but Primo continued, 'And, while we're being formal, allow me to introduce *Signorina* Galina Mantini.'

Out of the corner of her eye Olympia had just noticed a young woman coming towards them. Now she registered that this was the most astoundingly lovely creature she had ever seen. She seemed to be about eighteen, with honey-blonde hair that reached almost to her waist, and a flawless, peachy skin. She laid a possessive hand on Primo's arm, gazed at him adoringly and giggled.

'Galina, this is my brother, Luke, and his fiancée, Olympia.'

The glorious Galina put out her hand and said, '*Buon giorno,*' in a soft, ravishing voice.

Olympia pulled herself together to return the greeting. Outwardly controlled, inwardly she was hurt and angry. Her own sadness of the last few weeks suddenly seemed like a mockery. She'd thought his feelings were as deep as her own, when she'd merely been a passing fancy.

You should have known! How often had she said that about him? She hadn't been ready for this. But she ought to have been.

She was too preoccupied to notice Luke's eyes, flickering this way and that, bright with malicious interest. As they moved on into the house Luke gave his brother an understanding nod, which Primo met with a set, rigid face. But she didn't see that either.

Her parents seemed to be instinctively on everyone's wavelength, especially Grandpapa Rinucci, who seized on them with delight.

'What a fascinating man,' Angela said when she'd briefly escaped his clutches. 'Did you know he's actually seen Vesuvius erupt?'

'In 1944,' Luke said with a grin, 'soon after Italy was liberated. It lasted three days and he managed to grab a piece of lava as a souvenir. Ever since then he knows when the volcano is speaking to him personally. When anyone isn't telling the truth it sends a plume of smoke into the air.'

He said this like someone reciting words often recited before and Angela chuckled. 'You've heard it all before, haven't you?' she asked.

'Only about a thousand times,' Luke groaned.

'But we're really grateful to you,' said Toni, who was listening nearby. 'It's a long time since the old man had a brand new audience.'

Angela looked around her in delight, taking in the warmth of the whole family.

'You're so lucky,' she told Hope. 'So many sons and so good-looking.'

'But you too are lucky,' Hope said. 'The sadness of my life is that I didn't have a daughter. I would have liked one as much like yours as possible.' Then she added conspiratorially, 'But perhaps soon you will share her with me?'

Angela nodded, also conspiratorial.

'Sons are a great trial,' Hope confided. 'I have six, and how many have brought girls to their mother's party tonight? Only two.'

Her accusing gaze fell on Carlo, who reddened.

'Mamma—I did explain—'

'I do not wish to discuss it,' she informed him loftily. 'Except to say that I have heard of that incident, and you should be ashamed of yourself.'

'I am, Mamma,' he said unconvincingly.

Ruggiero, his twin, chimed in beside him. 'He is. He's very ashamed of himself. And I'm ashamed for him.'

Under his mother's withering glance he fell silent. When Hope was sure she'd reduced her menfolk to abject submission she turned back to Angela.

'You should give thanks you never had boys,' she told her. 'They are nothing but trouble. But at least two of my sons are behaving properly tonight.'

Her smiling glance included Luke and Olympia, then Primo and Galina. She seemed to be waiting for someone to say something. But nobody did. At last Ruggiero said, with the air of a man desperate to break the silence, 'Francesco is bringing his girlfriend tonight.'

'Good. At least one of you knows his duty. And there he is.'

She went forward to greet Francesco who had appeared with a pretty, modest-looking young woman. Hope made much of her, to the knowing grins of the others.

Dinner was a riot. Harold was seated next to Grandpapa Rinucci, who spoke good English which, as he would tell anyone who would listen, he'd learned from the Allies in 1944. That was when Vesuvius—

And Harold won his eternal friendship by saying, 'Tell me about Vesuvius. It's fascinating.' Just as if he hadn't heard it once already.

To the amusement of the others, they plunged into an animated discussion. Letting her eyes drift past them, Olympia saw Primo and Galina, their heads together, absorbed in each other. Or maybe it was her plunging neckline that absorbed him, she thought bitterly. He hadn't waited long before replacing her. She'd been right not to trust him.

Having taken centre stage, Grandpapa Rinucci flowered. 'And when are you coming back for the wedding?' he demanded of Angela.

'Which wedding?' she asked eagerly.

'Any wedding. Primo's to Galina, Luke's to Olympia. We should have more weddings.'

'Count me out,' Olympia said firmly. 'I'm concentrating on my career. In fact, I don't even believe in love.'

'Oh, darling, don't say things like that,' Angela begged. 'She doesn't mean it.'

'Yes, she does,' Olympia declared, desperate to seize the chance to say this. 'Love is a snare for the unwary. My career is all I want.'

Before anyone could answer, there was a soft rumbling in the distance. At once a silence descended on the entire company and their heads turned towards the window.

The rumbling came again, and with one movement they all rose and went out on to the terrace. In the distance a soft plume of smoke rose into the night air and disappeared.

'Is it going to erupt?' Angela asked, thrilled.

'No, these little grumbles happen a lot,' Hope reassured her. 'It means nothing.'

'Oh, yes, it does,' Grandpapa insisted. 'It means that someone—' his eyes lingered on Olympia '—is telling white lies. Or maybe black lies.'

'Or maybe she meant every word,' Olympia said, managing to laugh it off.

Right on cue Vesuvius growled deep in the ground and sent up another plume. Everyone laughed and there were knowing cries of 'Aha!'

The meal was almost over and nobody returned to the table. Seeing that her parents were happy, Olympia relaxed slightly. Now she could afford to think of herself and what had just happened. It was only a joke, not worth a moment's thought. She wasn't superstitious.

Suddenly Primo was beside her. 'May I refill that for you?' he asked, indicating her glass.

'No, I've had enough, thank you.'

He took the glass from her and set it down. 'You're looking very well,' he said politely.

'So are you. Are you back for good now?'

'No, just for a few days, then I'm going back to finish putting the new arrangements in place.'

'How is poor Cedric?'

'Enjoying his retirement. On his last evening we went out and got a little "drunk and disorderly" together.'

'You? Drunk and disorderly? Surely not?'

'I used to in my younger days.'

'That's hard to imagine, but I expect you planned it all beforehand, so much of this to drink, so much of that, always stay in charge of the situation.'

Primo gave a curt, mirthless laugh.

'You've just described my brother, not me. Luke's the cold, hard-headed one, planning everything to suit himself.'

'I haven't seen that in him.'

'No, he's different with you, I'll give him that. But if you make the mistake of marrying him you'll find out in the end.'

'Then the two of you are much the same,' she flung at him. 'Maybe that's why you're always at odds. It's a toss-up which of you is more determined to arrange life to suit himself.'

That got to him, she was glad to see. He flinched.

'I'm not as bad as you think.'

'Aren't you? Then tell me this. I've been thinking back and remembering that Cedric had met you before. He knew it was you all the time, didn't he?'

'Yes,' he admitted reluctantly.

'How did you persuade him to keep quiet? His pension didn't suddenly double, did it?'

'Not quite double.'

'So you bribed him, just like you bribed the hotel receptionist. You only have two ways of dealing with people, haven't you? Delude them, and bribe them. Did you ever try approaching anyone straightforwardly? Or don't you know how?'

'Olympia, please—'

'All right, I've finished. We don't need to talk any more.'

'So when is the announcement?'

'What announcement?'

'Of your engagement to my brother. Isn't that why your parents are here?'

'No, it's pure chance. They're just staying with us for a few days.'

'With us?'

'Staying at Luke's apartment.'

'I see.'

'No, you don't see. He said I could invite them while he was away but then he came back early.'

'Like a good prospective son-in-law. They love him. Your mother was telling me how wonderful he is, and your father longs for the day when he'll give you away.'

'And you heard what I said.'

'Yes, I did.' He gave a wry grin. 'So did Vesuvius, and you know what he thought of it.'

'Don't tell me you're superstitious.'

'You can't live here without being superstitious. The old man over the bay can tell when you're lying.'

'That's it. That's enough,' she said furiously. 'I spent weeks talking nonsense with you—'

'You should know. You did most of the talking.'

She breathed hard. 'I'm going back to join the others now,' she said, and walked away.

She shouldn't have talked to him. It had been a mistake, one that she wouldn't make again.

The party split into small groups to drink coffee. Hope was talking about her first son, Justin, snatched from her at birth.

'It will be the holidays soon and then perhaps Justin will return with my grandson,' she said, smiling at Olympia. 'And then you will meet him.'

'I'll really look forward to it,' Olympia said. 'I think it's wonderful how you found each other at last.'

'That's what Primo did for me,' Hope said, regarding him fondly. 'He gave me back my eldest son.'

'No, Mamma,' he said, looking uncomfortable. 'You can't give one person to another. If they find you it's because they want to. Justin was seeking you and in the end he would have found you himself.'

Olympia thought Hope was preparing to say more, but then she checked herself, as though she'd realised Primo wanted to end the subject.

'Is there any hope that we'll see Evie again?' Luke asked.

'I fear not,' Hope said sadly. To Olympia she explained, 'Evie is the woman who came here with him the first time. She'd done so much for him, and anyone could see that they loved each other, but now they seem to have broken up.'

'Then perhaps they did not love each other,' Toni pointed out.

'Why do you say that?' Olympia asked impulsively. 'Sometimes people love each other and still break up. It doesn't mean the love wasn't there, just that they couldn't find the path that led to each other.'

Hope made a sudden movement of interest. Several of the others turned to look at Olympia, but she couldn't see if Primo was one of them as her head was turned away from him. Even so, she sensed him grow still.

'I think you are right,' Hope said, nodding to her. 'I know that Justin is a difficult man. He says so himself. He wouldn't be an easy husband for any woman, but I think Evie could have been the right wife for him, if only—' She sighed.

'If only someone would help them,' Olympia said impulsively.

'You think so?' Hope asked. 'But how?'

'Talk to them, make them talk to each other. Knock their heads together.'

'If only—' Hope murmured. 'But then my family would say I was an interfering busybody.'

'Let them,' Olympia said robustly. 'People sometimes call me an interfering busybody, but I've never let it stop me yet.'

This caused a general laugh and Hope patted her hand.

'I knew there was a reason I like you so much,' she said triumphantly.

As the evening drew to a close Olympia sought refuge in the cool night air, from a position where she could glare at Vesuvius across the bay.

'You're a real pain in the butt,' she informed him. 'In future, shut up.'

He loomed in tactful silence. He'd had his fun.

It was a relief to be away from the chattering crowd. Her head was starting to ache from the confused impressions she had received tonight.

Primo's face was in her mind, pale and strained as she'd seen him in the first moment, then cool and smiling as he'd introduced his glamorous companion.

'Oh, it's nice to be out in the fresh air!'

It was Hope, further down the terrace, echoing Olympia's thoughts.

She was about to speak up when she heard Primo's voice, saying, 'Yes, come and sit down for a moment, Mamma. You're looking tired.'

'I am, but it's been a wonderful evening. Galina and Olympia are both so beautiful. I wonder when—'

'When we'll see Justin again,' he interrupted her quickly.

'Yes, that too. Every family party feels as though something is missing.' Hope sighed.

'But you used to say that before we found him,' he reminded her. 'Then he was truly missing. Now you know where he is, and that he will come here again soon.'

There was a silence, then Primo said, 'Are you thinking of what Olympia said?'

'Of course I am. It's so tempting to think that she was right, because then I'd have an excuse to act.'

'And you always like an excuse to act.'

The words were not said in criticism. Olympia could hear the fond humour in his voice.

'True, but I suppose my wise son would counsel caution?'

'You do me an injustice, Mamma. I think Olympia is right.'

'You, agreeing with Olympia? I thought you didn't like her, chiefly because she and Luke are in love.'

'You're wrong—' Primo sounded as though he'd been about to blurt something out, then checked himself. 'You're wrong, Mamma. I do not dislike her, and I think she'll make an admirable wife for Luke. But she's also a wise woman who's learned some hard lessons about love.'

'You sound as if you know her well.'

'I do know her, better than you think. Tonight she spoke to you out of her wisdom and her pain. You should listen to her. If Evie and Justin belong together then we should do everything possible to help them overcome whatever troubles them.'

'*You* say this?'

'That surprises you?'

'A little, because although it was you who found Justin, I don't think you feel like a brother to him.'

'That doesn't matter. I know now that to find the ideal person and then lose them because—'

Olympia heard him take a sharp breath and then go on with difficulty.

'Because of what?' Hope asked curiously.

'Because of their own foolishness, and because there was nobody to help them find the way that they had lost—it can happen too easily, and then the worst thing is to know that it was your own fault. I wouldn't wish it on any man. Not Justin. Not Luke.'

'Not yourself?' Hope asked gently.

Primo gave a curt laugh. 'I can take care of myself.'

'Can you, my son? I thought so once. Now I've begun to wonder. Once you seemed so strong—'

'I'm much stronger now, Mamma. A man is always better for making discoveries—especially about himself. From what you say, Justin has discovered many things, but they have left him confused. Olympia has spoken the truth. You must help him through that confusion.'

'And you? Are you confused?'

Primo spoke quietly. 'No, Mamma. My confusion is over. Now, come inside. It's getting chilly.'

Olympia didn't move but sat there silently until she knew that they had gone. She discovered that her face was wet, but she couldn't remember when she had started to weep.

As part of the *Maggio dei Monumenti* celebrations Enrico was laying on a ball for all the 'notables' as he called them. His guests included most of the Council of Naples, who organised the festival, the older Neapolitan families and many of his employees. This year the number of employees was greater and included many from England, to mark the successful merger.

He had persuaded Angela and Harold to extend their visit for a few days and join him. On the night they set off, with Luke and Olympia, for one of the local *palazzos,* now owned by the city, where he had hired the ballroom.

It was a grand occasion. The Rinuccis were there in force—Francesco with the girlfriend on whom Hope was pinning expectations, Primo escorting Galina, who looked like a model in a white satin dress that plunged down at the front, down at the back and up at the side. She had exactly the perfect figure to get away with it and Olympia reckoned that if Primo was making a point then he was doing it in style.

She herself was elegant in deep blue silk, but she was glad she hadn't worn white. She could never have competed with the luscious Galina.

Enrico was ebullient. The occasion had gone to his head and he was set on marking it symbolically. He gathered Primo and Olympia to him to receive directions.

'It will be a wonderful evening,' he enthused, 'and the culmination will be the moment when the two of you take the floor together for the waltz.'

'Surely that's not really necessary,' Olympia said.

'Of course it's necessary. We are celebrating the merger of our two firms, ushering in a time of peaceful co-existence, of happy union—'

'It's two firms not two kingdoms,' Olympia pointed out. 'Can we keep a sense of proportion?'

'I agree,' Primo said through gritted teeth. 'I think you should forget this idea.'

'I will not forget it,' Enrico spluttered, enraged. 'It is essential to tell the world of our blissful—'

'Well, I don't feel blissful,' Olympia said firmly. 'Why can't *you* dance with someone?'

'If I do, my wife kill me,' he said mournfully. 'No, it must be you.'

'No,' they both said together.

'What nonsense is this? I demand that you dance together.'

They yielded to placate him, and took the floor for the first dance.

'I'm sorry about this,' Primo growled.

'Don't worry. I'm getting to know Enrico's little ways by now. He's harmless. We only have to smile and be polite, then go our separate ways.'

'Our separate ways. Do you know how melancholy that sounds?'

'New roads always lead to something,' she reminded him.

'But suppose it isn't the place we want to go?'

'You have Galina waiting on your road. She'll probably take you somewhere interesting.'

'Shut up,' he said softly. 'Don't talk like that, do you hear me?'

'Why not? What difference can it make now?'

'You speak as if I'd betrayed you. But if you can say Galina, I can say Luke. Tell me that you're not in love with him. Let me hear you say it.'

'Didn't I once tell you that I never fall in love with unsuitable men?'

'Yes, and I asked what kind of man did you fall in love with. You said you couldn't remember. But that was then. This is now.'

'And life grows more complicated as time passes.'

'Witch,' he said bitterly. '*Strega.*'

'Yes, you should beware of me.'

His mouth was so close to hers that she could feel the whisper of his breath across her lips. The sense of sweet pleasure was so intense that she felt faint. She longed for him to kiss her, longed for it so intensely that nothing else mattered. She was swept by a desire to forget all her careful, self-protective plans and kiss him first.

At any moment she would do so and the world could think what it pleased—any moment—

The music slowed. It was over. People were applauding the dance that symbolised the creation of the new firm. In the midst of the applause Primo led her to Luke, inclined his head in a little bow and walked away, back to Galina.

The next morning they went their separate ways.

CHAPTER TWELVE

OLYMPIA saw her parents off at the airport.

'We've had such a lovely time, darling,' Angela said, 'and it'll be so lovely coming out for your wedding. Luke's a delightful young man, but don't you let the other one put a stop to it.'

'The other one—put a stop to it—?'

'Primo, the one who stands about scowling at you and Luke. Watch out for him, because he'll block it if he can.'

'I'll be careful,' Olympia promised. 'But don't count on my marrying Luke. Things aren't always what they seem.'

'Don't be silly, dear. I've seen the way he looks at you. Goodbye, now.'

Three days later there was news from England.

'Mamma's done it!' Luke announced triumphantly as he came off the phone. 'Don't ask me how, but she's made Justin and Evie see sense and the wedding's going to take place here, next month.'

Olympia spent an evening with Hope, who was happily deep in wedding plans. She had a natural gift for organising that was almost as great as Olympia's own, and soon the entire family had been turned into lieutenants, scurrying hither and thither at her command.

Justin, Evie and Justin's son, Mark, were to stay at the villa and arrived two days early.

'I know it's not usual for the bride and groom to start from the same house,' Hope said to Olympia, 'but neither of them has a home here, and this way I can keep an eye on them.'

'You're afraid they're going to escape you again,' Olympia teased. Hope laughed and didn't deny it.

Toni and Primo, newly returned from England, went with her to the airport to greet them, and that evening everyone congregated at the villa. Olympia was immediately taken by Evie's wit and her ready laugh, which obviously covered a sharp intelligence. Justin was an interesting man, apparently harsh, yet seeming to cling to Evie. If she left his side his eyes followed her around the room.

Mark was already a favourite with the family and now he won Olympia's heart with his cheeky antics and his happiness at being there. After Hope, he was the person most anxious for the marriage to take place without delay.

'He's a bit like Primo, when I married his father, Jack Cayman,' Hope confided. 'He wanted a mother so badly. I'll never forget the way he smiled when he finally felt certain of me.'

But that certainty had proved an illusion, Olympia thought. His 'mother' had been taken from him and, although she had been restored later, he'd never felt completely safe again.

Hope's use of the name Jack Cayman brought a host of other memories back. Now she saw how Primo's early experiences had shaped him. Beneath the apparently solid self-confidence was something rootless, constantly mobile, as though he were seeking something that could never be found.

It didn't take much insight to deduce that much the same was true of Justin, whose life had been built on even greater confusion.

Snatched from his mother at birth, he had later been rejected by his adoptive parents and abandoned in an institution. He'd reached manhood angry and bitter, caring for nobody, ready to do anything.

Against all the odds he'd made something of his life and was now a wealthy man and the head of a huge firm. But the scars remained and they had made him reject Evie, who loved him, for her sake. Now, thanks to Hope's intervention, things had come right for them, and the whole family had joined to wish them well.

Since Primo had been the one to find him first, Justin had asked him to be his best man. Toni was to give the bride away as Evie had no family. And the day before the wedding Olympia's parents arrived, at Hope's invitation, the clearest signal that she was still plotting.

On the morning of the wedding the entire Rinucci family gathered at the villa, which made an impressive sight. Some were staying there, some had travelled up early in the morning, until at last everyone was there.

Galina, as always, was a knockout in a light blue chiffon dress that contrived to be fairly restrained, for church, while leaving no doubt about her glorious figure. Olympia's honey-coloured linen, which had seemed so elegant in the mirror, now looked dull. In fact, she told herself that she looked almost middle-aged beside Galina's vibrant youth.

Primo noticed her and drew Galina across for a greeting. The morning sun flashed off something around the girl's neck, which closer inspection proved to be a gold chain with heavy, elaborate links.

'Isn't it beautiful?' Galina squealed when Olympia admired it.

'Did Primo give you that?' Luke asked.

Galina just giggled. Olympia stared out of blank eyes. A gift so valuable was a declaration of intent.

'It's time the groom was leaving for the church,' Hope said, bustling over. 'And those of you who are going with him, the car's ready outside.'

Justin appeared, dreadfully pale, and was taken in charge by Primo. A few minutes later the two of them departed together, with Galina.

More cars were lined up before the house; people started checking themselves in the mirror, taking care of last minute details.

Then everyone was silenced by the arrival of the bride. Evie had chosen a simple ivory-coloured dress with a short veil held in place by flowers. She looked beautiful, but she also looked honest, calm and strong. In fact she was exactly what the man she loved most needed.

And Hope knew it, because she gave her new daughter a special mother's embrace before taking her hand and putting it in Toni's.

'You will give her away,' she said, smiling, 'and then she will be ours.'

No bride could have asked for a better welcome, Olympia thought as she and Luke headed out to the cars. But she knew now that it could never be hers. There could be no marriage between herself and Luke, whatever other people thought, and it was time for her to leave.

His brotherly kindness had lulled her into a sense of security and she had lingered too long. But now it was time to depart and set a distance between herself and the Rinucci family. That way she need no longer see Primo with Galina.

But then she thought of working with him, seeing him day after day, and knew that mov-

ing home wasn't enough. She must go away
entirely, back to England, to another job. It
would mean starting again.

But I can do that, she thought. I've done it
before.

The wedding ceremony was an impressive
ritual, but the most impressive part was when
two people claimed each other with quiet fer-
vour. Then the organ pealed out and they
started back down the aisle into the sunlight,
where the photographer was waiting.

So many photographs to be taken, so many
family combinations. Nobody must be left out,
and Olympia found herself kindly dragooned
into many pictures where she felt she had no
right to be. But Hope was determined and nobody could stand up to her.

'Not if they want to live,' Luke commented
wryly.

Then the formal reception, the speeches,
Justin almost inarticulate, having to be rescued
by his son, saying cheekily, 'Dad hasn't got
much Italian yet, so I'll do it.'

At last the tables were cleared for dancing.
Olympia watched the bride and groom, stand-

ing well back against the wall, a glass of champagne in her hand.

'Making plans?' Primo's voice asked ironically.

'Oh, shut up,' she said, abandoning tact.

'But how much longer can you keep us all on tenterhooks while you delay the announcement? Soon you will be my sister-in-law—or you would be, if I acknowledge that *Inglese* as a brother.'

'Primo, will you please stop talking nonsense? Of course I'm not going to marry Luke.' She faced him, suddenly angry and too full of regret to care much what she said. 'How could you ever have believed it for one minute?'

'Because you went to live with him.'

'Only because I was angry with you. You should have known that. You *did* know it. Where have your wits been all this time?'

He stared at her. 'This is my fault?'

She thought of Galina and sadness overcame her.

'No, mine too, I suppose. I wasn't very clever from the start, or I'd have seen through you.' She gave a wry smile. 'Let's face it, you didn't really do it very well. You didn't fool me. I fooled myself. I wanted to believe in my own cleverness. I've nobody to blame but me, so I think we should part friends and forget it ever happened.'

'Friends?' he murmured, and then, '*Part?*'

'Yes, I'm leaving. It's time this was over. I'm going back to England.'

He stared at her, seemingly unable to think of a reply. When it came it wasn't the one he would have chosen.

'You can't. You've got a contract.'

'Sue me.'

She turned and began to walk away, moving out on to the terrace. But he came after her and pulled her round to face him.

'People will see,' she said frantically.

'Let them. It's time we had this out. You've been playing me for a sucker for far too long.'

'*I've* been—?'

'Everything you've done recently has been done to punish me. Living with that *Inglese,* making my whole family see you as a couple. You were teaching me a lesson, weren't you? I thought better of you.'

'Oh, don't give me that,' she said angrily. 'We both behaved badly. We both thought better of the other, and we were both disappointed.'

'Which seems to leave us about even,' he said, giving her a curious look.

'Yes.' She sighed. 'And that's a good place to finish.'

'Are you sure about that?' he asked, looking at her strangely. 'Some people might say it was a good place to start.'

'What?'

'Don't you realise that what you've been saying for the past few minutes gives us the best chance we've ever had? Olympia, for the first time we can be honest with each other. That's a great start.'

There was a gleam far back in his eyes that obscurely disturbed her, but she refused to take any notice. She had made her decision and this time she would stick to it.

'I can't believe you're saying this. After what we did to each other—'

'That was bad, and we needed some time apart to get over it, but we've had that and now we're ready—'

'Will you stop telling me what to do?'

'Somebody needs to, because you're lost and confused. Almost as lost and confused as I am, but this is where it stops. Tell me that you love me.'

She gasped in outrage. '*Is that an order?*'

'Yes, it is! And look sharp about it, I'm tired of waiting.'

'The devil I will!' she said, trying to turn away again.

'The devil you won't,' he said, pulling her back. 'Now listen to me. I stood there in that church, watching Justin and Evie and wondering how I'd ever let things go this wrong.'

'But so did I—'

'Then tell me that you love me.'

'Now, look here—'

'Say it—'

Before she knew it his lips were against hers and his arms about her.

'Say it,' he muttered.

'I'm blowed if I—'

'*Say it!*'

But in the same instant he made it impossible for her to say anything, kissing her until she was breathless and incapable of thought.

She had deadened herself to emotions, not once but twice—first for David and then, recently, trying to kill her love for Primo. But now the sweet, uncontrollable feelings rose up and refused to die down.

She loved him. She might deny it from now until kingdom come, but it would still be true.

'Say it,' he murmured again. 'Or I'll kiss you forever until you do.'

'In that case, my lips are sealed.'

He was laughing, his body shaking, sending tremors through her too.

'I love you, I love you,' she said. 'But don't stop.'

All tension and sadness seemed to melt away in kiss after kiss. She was only distantly aware of a door opening and closing behind her, but then she felt Primo draw back a little in dismay.

'Well, well,' said Luke's voice.

Shocked, she whirled and saw him standing there, leaning against the wall, regarding them both with apparent amusement.

'So you reached the finishing line at last,' he said. 'I thought you would if I was patient.'

'You—?' she said uncertainly. 'You mean you—all this time—?'

'I think I've been rather clever,' Luke said with a grin that might have been aimed against himself. 'That first night, when you got mad and wanted to leave, I had to find a way to keep you in Naples—'

'Why?' Primo asked at once.

Luke gave a crack of derisive laughter.

'Because I knew she was the one woman who could bring you down, of course. And I wasn't going to miss the fun. And has it ever been fun! The sight of you not knowing whether you were coming or going has been the best laugh I've ever had. I've seen jealousy on your face that you could barely control. I've seen you driving yourself crazy because you wanted something you couldn't arrange to have, and you couldn't even admit it to yourself. Did I enjoy that? You bet I did!'

Primo began to swear softly under his breath. Olympia couldn't follow the names he called his brother, but they must have been outrageous because Luke relished every one of them.

'Don't!' Olympia got diplomatically between them. 'Don't let anything spoil it now. Primo, whatever his reasons, your brother did us a favour.'

'Don't call him my brother—'

'Of course he's your brother,' she insisted. 'Only a brother would do you a huge favour and insult you afterwards, and then laugh at you and with you—'

'You're going to be a good influence on him,' Luke observed. 'You could even knock some of the nonsense out of him.'

'Luke, you were never in love with me, were you?' she asked hopefully.

He shrugged. 'Maybe just a bit. But not enough to worry about. I've been a perfect gentleman so that you could stay here without worry, and it all worked out right.' He grinned suddenly. 'Mind you, there might be a problem. Your mother likes me better.'

'I'll bet she does,' Primo murmured. He still eyed Luke askance, but he was calming down.

Olympia kissed Luke's cheek and was enfolded in a brotherly hug. As he turned to go, Primo called, '*Hey, Inglese!*'

He waited until Luke looked back before saying quietly, 'Thank you.'

'Hah! You think you've won, but she'll lead you a merry dance, and I'll be there, laughing all the way. Starting with the altar. I want to be your best man.'

'I wouldn't have anyone else.'

Luke walked away.

'Yes, I think I've won,' Primo said. 'I *know* I've won. I've won everything I want in the world.'

He seized her in his arms again. Neither of them saw Luke turning at the last minute. He watched them for a moment, then touched his cheek where Olympia had kissed it and murmured, 'Maybe just a bit.'

Olympia's conscience was troubling her.

'What about Galina? You weren't trying to make me jealous, surely?'

'No, because I didn't think I could. I wanted to save my face, so that when you and Luke announced your engagement I wouldn't be standing there alone like a lemon.'

'But if she's in love with you—'

That made him roar with laughter.

'My darling, as far as Galina's concerned I'm an old man. She's eighteen. I only know her because her parents are friends of mine. When she found out what was happening—and it's hard to keep anything from that girl—she said, "What you need is window-dressing, Uncle Primo, and I'm the person to help you." So I turned up with her on my arm, just to save my dignity. She came to my rescue again after that, but she'll be glad it's over so that she can go back to boys of her own age.'

'She doesn't really call you uncle?'

'I swear she does. She kept coming out with it all that evening, and I had to keep frantically reminding her not to. Let's find her so that I can tell her that she's off duty from now on.'

They found Galina a few moments later, dancing smoochily with Ruggiero, so absorbed in him that it was with great difficulty that Primo attracted her attention. Then he pointed to Olympia, giving a thumbs up sign. Galina smiled, waved and touched the heavy gold chain about her neck. Then she hooked an arm around Ruggiero's neck and forgot all about Uncle Primo.

As they walked away, Primo said, 'What did you think of the chain—my thank you gift?'

'Very pretty.'

'Wait until you see the one I will buy you.'

In another room Luke found solitude and a bottle of good whisky.

There Hope discovered him a few minutes later.

'I saw what happened,' she said fondly. 'It's what you were planning all the time, isn't it? You always knew it would be Olympia and Primo in the end.'

'I guess I did. But Mamma, sometimes you have to ask yourself, if a man acts like such a clown when he's wooing his woman, isn't another man entitled to step in and—?' He finished with a shrug.

'So why didn't you?' she asked, holding out a glass for Luke to pour her a whisky.

'I nearly did. There were nights when I stood outside her bedroom door while my worse and better selves fought it out. My worse self put up a brave fight—'

'But your better self always won?'

'Unfortunately, yes,' he said savagely, and she laughed.

Then he sighed. 'It wouldn't have been any use. Primo's the one for her, I could see that.'

'So you played Cupid. I always knew that you were really a good brother.'

'Don't say that,' he said hurriedly. 'Think of my reputation.'

Hope laughed. 'All right, I'll keep quiet about it. But we both know the truth, which is that you have a kind heart, a *brother's* heart.'

He grimaced. 'Yes, it's just a shame that it asserted itself now, and about *her*.'

'Somewhere there is a woman for you. You'll get over Olympia.'

'Sure I will—say, in about a hundred years. In the meantime, perhaps I'd better go away for a while.'

'Far?' Hope asked in alarm.

'No, only as far as Rome. A man there owed me quite a lot of money. He couldn't pay so he signed over some property he owned. It's likely to prove more of a curse than a blessing, as I gather it's in a bad way. There have been no improvements to speak of for a long time, and there's a lawyer giving him grief. He describes her as the devil incarnate, which means she'll give me grief as well.'

'She?'

'*Signora* Minerva Pepino. I've already had a letter from her that practically took the skin off my back.'

'Good. She'll keep your mind occupied.' She kissed him. 'Go to Rome, my son, and come back for Primo's wedding. Perhaps you will bring a bride home of your own.'

'I doubt it. Be content with two daughters-in-law, Mamma.'

'Nonsense. I want six. Now, come back and join the party.'

She departed, humming. After a moment Luke followed her and stood, unnoticed, watching the revelry. Justin was dancing with his bride, his harsh face softened by happiness. Primo circled the floor with Olympia, both enclosed in their own cocoon of joy.

Luke watched her and knew that she had forgotten him.

'I had to go and be a ''good brother'', didn't I?' he groaned. 'It was bound to happen one day, but in heaven's name, why now?'

He stood for a moment watching Primo and Olympia—soon to be his sister—held close in each other's arms, absorbed and happy.

'Why now?' he murmured.

The wedding was over. The house was sleeping, except for the two in the gardens. It was dark out there, except for the moon, and the only sound was of two lovers whispering.

'I never meant to lie to you,' he vowed, 'but the moment we met I knew you had to be mine. I'd lived such a safe, sensible life, but none of that meant anything after I saw you. I wanted to be wild and even stupid.'

'Well, you were certainly that,' she told him fondly.

'Are you going to be a nagging wife?'

'One of me is. The others haven't decided.'

'Ah yes,' he said, understanding her at once. 'We'll always have that now. An infinite variety—very handy for playing away—'

'Planning to be unfaithful, huh?'

'Only with you, *amor mio*. Only with you.'

Her deep, delighted chuckle brought the world to life. In the moonlight he saw her pulling at her hair, becoming a witch before his eyes.

'You know this one, don't you?' she teased. 'It's the corny film where the heroine lets her hair fall loose and the hero goes weak at the knees, and swears to love her for ever.'

'Yes,' he said, taking her joyfully into his arms. 'That's exactly what happens…'

MILLS & BOON® PUBLISH EIGHT LARGE PRINT TITLES A MONTH. THESE ARE THE EIGHT TITLES FOR MAY 2006

THE SHEIKH'S INNOCENT BRIDE
Lynne Graham

BOUGHT BY THE GREEK TYCOON
Jacqueline Baird

THE COUNT'S BLACKMAIL BARGAIN
Sara Craven

THE ITALIAN MILLIONAIRE'S VIRGIN WIFE
Diana Hamilton

HER ITALIAN BOSS'S AGENDA
Lucy Gordon

A BRIDE WORTH WAITING FOR
Caroline Anderson

A FATHER IN THE MAKING
Ally Blake

THE WEDDING SURPRISE
Trish Wylie

MILLS & BOON®

Live the emotion

0406 Rom

MILLS & BOON® PUBLISH EIGHT LARGE PRINT TITLES A MONTH. THESE ARE THE EIGHT TITLES FOR JUNE 2006

THE HIGH-SOCIETY WIFE
Helen Bianchin

THE VIRGIN'S SEDUCTION
Anne Mather

TRADED TO THE SHEIKH
Emma Darcy

THE ITALIAN'S PREGNANT MISTRESS
Cathy Williams

FATHER BY CHOICE
Rebecca Winters

PRINCESS OF CONVENIENCE
Marion Lennox

A HUSBAND TO BELONG TO
Susan Fox

HAVING THE BOSS'S BABIES
Barbara Hannay

MILLS & BOON®

Live the emotion

0506 Rom LP